Still Dreaming California

Still Dreaming

California

Scenic Point

Adventure Stories

Laurie Anderson Hennig

Still Dreaming California

Written and Illustrated by

Laurie Anderson Hennig

*

Edited with the help of

Donna Stewman, Daniel Hennig & Linda Levy

First published in 2022

IBSN   9798797731139

A Camp Climax Production

P.O. Box 784, Boulder Creek, California 95006

Still Dreaming California

Angelo De Carli, an immigrant from Switzerland and a prosperous dairy farmer in the Carmel Valley married Jessie Machado in 1888. Her father, Christian Machado of the San Carlos Mission Ranch, had led a Papal inquiry to the grave of Father Junipero Serra within the mission in 1882. Their daughter Mary Josephine De Carli remembers growing up playing among the old adobe walls remaining around the Mission during reconstruction. Moving to Salinas in 1927, the De Carli family began a lifelong friendship with the neighboring Anderson family. Because of her historical knowledge, Josephine was a witness at the beatification trials for Father Junipero Serra at the Carmel Mission in 1949.

Dedicated to my Aunties

Arline Jane Anderson

and

Josephine De Carli-Cornett

Monterey County, California

They kept history alive
through their stories of early California

Still Dreaming California

Still Dreaming California

Table of Contents

Always Forward 1
El Camino Real 11
Punta Don Juan 24
A Moment in San Ignacio 38
Mulege Heroico 44
Bahia de Conception 53
Tropic of Cancer 58
Todos Santos: A Nuclear Wave 65
Santiago 77
Espectaculares! 84
Dancing on the Edge 89
Seeds of Change 102
Learning to Fly 112
Forgotten Relics 119
The Two Timers 129
Oasis 136
Cowgirl 146
Ports of Illusion 154
Lords of the Wind 164
Path of Miracles 173
La Frontera 187
Padre California 198
Appendix 211

*Spanish words are italicized

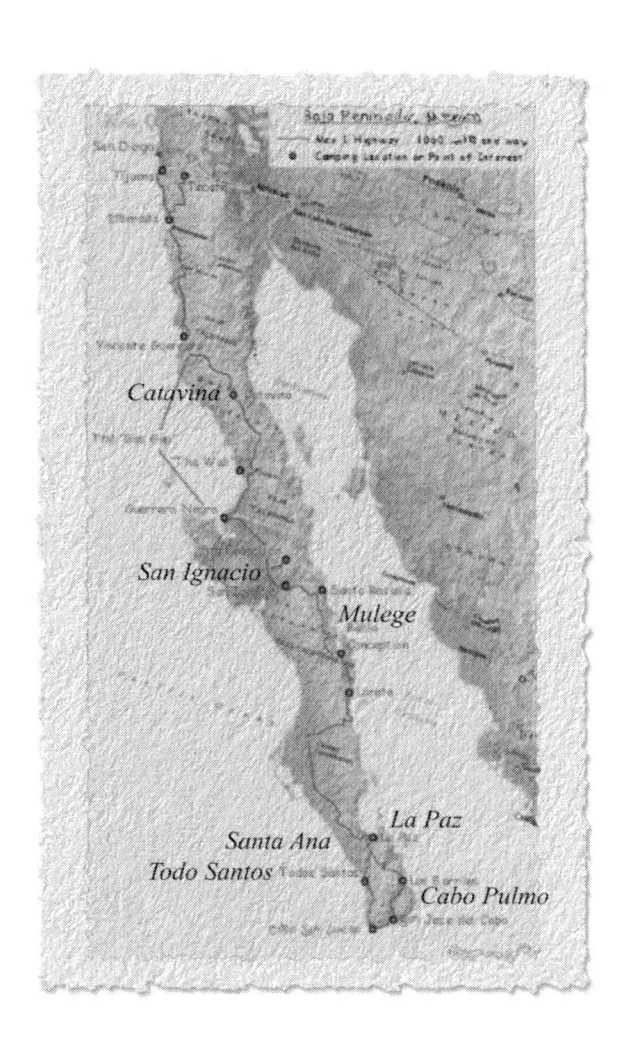

Still Dreaming California

Always Forward

A Sacred Expedition

The dog with the funny black behind continued it's mauling of a dead dove, tossing it playfully into a rising cloud of dust. It was a moment of destiny as the heat of an early November 1768 day settled over the *Sierra de las Lagunas* mountains and the remote Villa de Santa Ana where a small, shrouded figure was hunched over a big table in the shade of the broad patio of a stately manor. Prominently overlooking the sandy arroyo of *Agua Blanca*, the mansion was a proud reminder of civilization amidst the wild landscapes of *Baja California*. *Vaqueros* with weather beaten hats they called *sombreros* and dusty chaps called *armas*, were standing watch over horses and cattle dozing along the dry riverbed of *Agua Blanca*, ready for *siesta* time after a hot morning of roundup. *Padre* Junipero Serra had been summoned by the Viceroy of New Spain for a grand venture. Thinking about his recent voyage from Loreto, remembering the walk up that sandy arroyo from the landing place, the *Surgidero*, the *Padre* found himself romanticizing about the brave souls whose historical footsteps he was following.

First discovered by Spanish explorer Hernando Cortez, California had been claimed for Spain in 1533. Likening it to the fabled island of riches described in a 1510 Spanish novel about an empire of super women, mystique prevailed. Even after later exploration by Juan Rodriguez Cabrillo in 1542 and Sebastian Vizcaino in 1596, had identified California as a peninsula and not an island as originally thought by Cortez, it continued to be fatefully associated with golden promise.

Founded on the peninsula in 1697 by Jesuit Padre Juan Maria de Salvatierra, the heart of the mission colony was in Loreto along the rocky shore of the Sea of Cortez. The early Jesuits had laid out the missions from there, with the goal of changing the natives from heathen hunter-gatherers to Christian village farm dwellers growing food for community development. Seeking no personal gain, Jesuit philosophy had determined that all California land belonged to the converts they called *neophytes* and their goal had always been to guard and conserve it in trust for them through their power as a Theocracy. Their plan had included isolation of California, allowing no commerce or development of natural resources except as they benefited the missions and the natives communally.

Connected by the *Camino Real*, the missions were always located at water resources. Once developed, the path to the next water location and its local inhabitants was extended by converts to connect a new mission with its nearest older establishment. *Pueblos* gradually evolved around those missions, eventually creating competition for labor and scarce natural resources. During the early period of development, the Jesuit missions had been exempted from taxes and growing resentment of the theocratic monopoly eventually became the source of change.

Don Manuel de Ocio from Spain was *Antigua California's* first successful entrepreneur. A Spanish adventurer, a *gente de razon* as educated Europeans were called, he had been a soldier on *Loreto's* payroll in 1733 and had become the son-in-law to the *Capitano* by 1736. When a massive storm cast up a vast wealth of pearl oysters in 1741, the native *Cochimi* Tribes along the coast had gathered the pearls and Ocio had made the most of the opportunity. Buying and trading pearls to create a fortune for himself, he initiated a secular economy that began to challenge the power of the missions.

The trail from the Sea of Cortez landing, the *Surgidero* on the gulf shore opposite *Isla Cerralvo,* followed the river *arroyos* to the Pacific missions, passing through a mountain area known as *Santa Ana.* As a soldier escort, Manuel de Ocio had become familiar with the area and had recognized signs of mining potential. Although the area was in an unfriendly *Uchiti* territory, by 1748 Don Ocio had enlisted help from his brother-in-law, Pedro de la Riva, *Commandante* of the *Baja* troops and together had killed and exiled the indigenous natives and laid claim to the territory. Ocio was determined to create a new economic order in *California* and the *Villa de Santa Ana* became the first civilian settlement. Continually petitioning the *Viceroy* of New Spain, promising new sources of revenue for the Crown through ranching and mining projects, Don Ocio eventually won concessions for a new secular arrangement, awarding him land grants and forcing the missions to share water and grazing rights in order to support rising entrepreneurial endeavors.

When Carlos III inherited the throne of Spain in 1759, the European powers at that time were in an expansionist competition for resources, especially in the New World. Russian and French explorers were making their way down the Pacific coast, closing in on areas of *Alta California* already claimed by earlier Spanish explorers. So in 1767, anxious to secure his domain and impatient with the slow progress of Jesuit mission building, amid suspicions of hidden wealth, Carlos III expelled the Jesuit Order from all of *New Spain* (Mexico) and replaced them the following year with friars from the Franciscan order.

By early 1768, a seven-decade Jesuit theocracy in *Baja California* was over. Through relentless petitioning of the King for pearling rights, then mining rights and land grants with the promise of a wealth of taxes to be gained through civil governance, the ambitious entrepreneur Don Manuel de Ocio had accomplished an historic coup, igniting a quest for expansion and bringing Capitalism to *California*.

Pausing to gaze north, the *Padre* fixated for a moment on the thrusting boulders of *Mt. Ballena* where the heat of midday had created the illusion of ripples on a sea of breaching whales. Surrounded by tipped peaks of granite block, the *Sierra de las Lagunas* were green at that elevation, a little cooler and very different from the coastal desert scape he'd been surveying all summer.

With the exception of the comfortable mansion where they were staying, the primitive community of *Santa Ana* amounted to just a few scattered *casitas* surrounding mine shafts which littered the pocked sides of *Mt. Ballena* like open wounds. A desperate assortment of inhabitants was testament to the hardships endured in settling early *California* and it was obvious to the *Padre* that the vision of *Santa Ana* was not yet realized. And it wasn't just the *Ville de Santa Ana*. Serra and the *Franciscans* brothers that had arrived with him, had been in *California* long enough to inspect all of the missions, where they had witnessed the same desperate conditions.

Spain was ready to consolidate and expand its empire. Initiating a reorganization of their colonial territories, King Carlos III had appointed Jose de Galvaz, *Visitador Generalisimo* of New Spain, charging him with economic development and reforms in taxation. In addition, a meeting in *Santa Ana* had been called to solidify plans for an expedition of conquest.

Junipero Serra's zeal and stamina evangelizing in New Spain, had ordained him as the new *Padre Presidente* of the *California* missions already established by Jesuit Friars during the previous century. The *Padre* had been called from the mission headquarters at Loreto to *Santa Ana* by Galvaz to help with the planning for the Expedition.

Questing for legendary treasure, King Carlos III had high expectations, but for the humble Friar the legend translated into souls. Recently arrived with twelve other *Franciscans* from the college of *San Fernando* near Mexico City, they were there to take over and expand the missions after the expulsion of the Jesuits the previous year. The Franciscan plan was to bring Christianity to the "*pitiful people*" in the path of conquest, those indigenous populations living without Jesus. Aggravated by the brutality of military usurpation since the expulsion of the Jesuits, already following general neglect from the Spanish Crown, the native populations that hadn't already run away were now reduced to near starvation. With that scenario, complicated by recent drought, a pandemic, locusts and crop failure, the *Padre Presidente* was beginning to understand that they had probably all arrived with un-realistic expectations. For Junipero Serra, it was to be a *Sacred Expedition*.

Suddenly interrupted by the commotion of a stampede of new arrivals, a young bull abruptly charged out of a swirling pillar of dust, mounting the stairs onto the patio where the *Padre* was drafting plans. Skinny and covered with spiky *choya* cactus it was another reminder of the poor condition of the remaining mission livestock. Driving the half-starved beast away from the table of documents, he had to wonder if the poor creature was even worth the effort of round-up.

"The herds will be stronger by Spring" he could only hope. In preparation for the Expedition, the *Generalisimo* was requisitioning livestock from the miserable mission herds.

Returning his attention to "God's work", the *Padre* continued to sift through a yellowed stack of parchments, historic records of *California*. Detailed charts and maps of earlier explorations had identified good harbors along the Pacific coast of *California* and more recent explorations by Fernando de Rivera of Loreto had identified a path north by land.

Generalisimo Galvaz had already revealed his plan for a two-pronged expedition of conquest; "Two by land and two by sea" he had explained. They would begin the expedition in early spring and meet first in *San Diego* and eventually converge in *Monte Rey*.

With twenty-five years of experience in *California*, *Capitano* Fernando de Rivera y Moncada would lead the first part of the land expedition, leaving in the spring with the herds and some supplies to blaze the trail.

The Jesuit expulsion from California had been carried out by a new Military Governor, Gaspar de Portola and he had also been appointed by the Spanish Viceroy as *Commandante* of the Expedition. Recently from Catalonia, Spain, he was a good organizer and popular leader. Junipero Serra enjoyed his company. He was to be the leader of the second of the land expeditions, even though he was unfamiliar with the terrain and Serra would accompany him.

Two sea voyages, the *San Antonio* and the *San Carlos*, would be dispatched with troops and supplies, to be reinforced later by a third ship, the *San Jose*. The plan was to join the combined expeditions in *San Diego*, where they would begin the extended chain of *Alta California* missions and civilian cities.

Carefully spreading out the old parchment map and resting his finger on *Monte Rey*, that point of destiny, the *Padre* chorused a hopeful prayer, harmonizing with bird song drifting in from the surrounding *tierra*. A pair of Scrub Jays were darting through nearby low foliage and early migratory birds were collecting nesting materials.

"God willing... tweet, tweeeet" he mimicked. Junipero was known for his impulsively sweet voice and moving sermons, and the birds were welcome companions.

Serra was also famous for his physical stamina, but at age 56 he realized that this expedition was also going to be a challenge for him. A leg injury suffered on the journey to his new duties in *California* was making it painful to even walk.

Suddenly transfixed by the corpse of the dead dove flung through the air by the funny little dog, he determinedly sat up a little straighter on his chair.

"Even though I should die on the way, I shall not turn back." Junipero Serra pledged to follow the path with heart. "Always forward!" This was all God's will.

🌹

During the time between the expulsion of the Jesuits and the arrival of the Franciscans, the military had been in control, much to the detriment of the missions. The soldiers had abused their position, stealing, vandalizing, cutting the herds and inflicting "*immoral behavior*" on the converts, leaving the missions in "*wretched*" condition. Some missions had even been nearly abandoned and would have to be repopulated with *neophytes* from other missions.

Jose Galvez was a man of the Enlightenment. Like the King, he was skeptical of religion, imagining Spanish/Indian secularized settlements in a new prosperous *California*. So, it was ironic that the Sacred Expedition would have to rely on mission resources, of which *Padre Presidente* Serra was willing, but only with important concessions.

The *Padre Presidente* was understanding, "*these were difficult times*", but for his cooperation he wanted the kind of authority over the military that the Jesuits had enjoyed. Serra hoped for full control over his converts and was pressing for laws that would protect the natives against further abuses by Spanish soldiers.

Realizing that his plans for the occupation would need resources from the missions, the *Visitator General* promised to at least restore temporal responsibilities to the Franciscans. A military *escolta* would be assigned to guard and protect each mission and the communities would be subject to civil governance, but the spiritual Fathers would eventually have authority over new Christian converts, which importantly needed to include protection from military abuse.

In addition to his planning for the Expedition, Galvaz had committed to an ambitious agenda which included setting up civilian government and promoting economic development in *Baja California*. His *"laborius genius"* had been designing a new layout for *Santa Ana* since his arrival in July. Streets had been staked out and since many trees had been sacrificed to process ore, new trees were being planted to shade the developing community. His plan included a new chapel and he had ordered a thousand *pesos* given towards its establishment. Serra was humbly grateful, even as he understood the pivotal importance of the missions to this historic venture.

In addition to cutting the mission herds, already greatly depleted since the expulsion of the Jesuits, *Vaqueros* and gear would then have to be recruited to manage the round-up and stampede of the animals on the Expedition. Tanning would need to become a commercial enterprise in order for the missions to prosper in the new economy. They would be introducing agricultural methods and irrigation techniques, bringing seeds of change, wheat, beans, cabbages, fruit cuttings, olives and all the necessary farming implements. Vineyards and orchards would be planted. Wax, wicks and oils were being collected. Architectural projects would require carpentry and masonry tools and skills. Crafts would be taught to the converts.

With the invasion that was being organized, a wave of change was on the way to *Nueva California* and the natives would have to adapt to the new standards of private enterprise under Spanish rule. It was the Mission Fathers who would be expected to prepare the natives for the new system of *encomienda;* essentially forced labor as tribute to their new rulers.

In order to create the pomp necessary to impress and convert the *gentiles* that they would be encountering, church vestments, paintings and altar accouterments would have to be allotted from the existing *Baja* missions and shared with the new mission communities. Mass would need to become a spectacle and Junipero Serra knew how to make that happen. Well known for his musical abilities, choirs would be trained to glorify; Mass was his doorway into the Spirit.

Tentatively pushing his finger along a thin line running north through the *California* peninsula, following the route until he found *San Diego* on the old parchment map: That would be the first mission, followed by settlements along an extended *El Camino Real*. Moving further north along the coast, he noted the harbors of *Los Angeles* and *Santa Barbara*. These would be among the new mission settlements along with those others he would found along the way to *Monte Rey*.

The dog had left the mangled corpse of the dove with the *Padre* to go beg scraps in the *cocina,* where savory smells announced preparations for the mid-day meal. The *Generalisimo* had requisitioned Don Ocio's mansion in *Santa Ana* as his headquarters and they set a good table. The *Padre* wasn't convinced that they should be eating so well while the rest of the general population suffered so greatly, He realized though, that the *"high capacity of the Generalisimo"* justifiably needed to be sustained.

"We will take possession of the land claimed by Cabrillo in 1542. *Generalisimo* Galvaz was ambitiously explaining his plan to Governor Portola as they approached from the brilliance of the *arroyo* where they had left their horses with one of the mission *vaqueros*.

" And protect *California* from the ambitious designs of foreign nations" he continued with resolve. The *Padre* already knew that he was referring to Russian and increasing immigration from the East Coast States of North America.

The vultures were starting to circle as Governor Portola respectfully accompanied the *Viceroy*, climbing the broad stairs leading to the patio where the *Padre Presidinte* awaited them, completing the triad that would be finalizing plans for the historic invasion. Dwarfed by the physical stature of his companions, the determined *Padre* was nonetheless resolute as they joined him over the table to follow the proposed path of the *Sacred Expedition*. The trusted *Padre* Francisco Palou would be left in charge of the *Baja* missions while Serra accompanied the expedition with Portola.

"Always forward, never back. That will be my motto for this Expedition" the Padre fatefully pledged.

Determining locations along the California coastline for Spanish development, their intentions were strong.

Beyond the horizon of majestic mountains surrounding them, beyond, to where the *Sierra de las Lagunas* disappeared into hazy purple promise, they were dreaming of *a Nueva California*. A new Spanish California along an extended *El Camino Real* leading north to "*the pitiful people*". With no way of knowing the changes that were being designed for them, Spain would be seizing their treasure and if they accepted the Spanish King, their lives would be spared.

The Franciscans would be collecting their souls. Junipero Serra was certain that only Jesus could save them now.

El Camino Real

El Camino Real, The King's Highway, runs through the current of *California*. Following the ancient paths of the indigenous, it was originally developed south and then north from *Loreto* for the kings of Spain by waves of Jesuits seeking souls and land for an expanding New Spain. The highway was eventually extended by order of King Carlos III by Franciscans in 1769, to *San Diego* and then further north to *Monte Rey* the next year. Blazed by Gaspar de Portola and the Franciscan *Padre* Junipero Serra, later pilgrims followed the path of that "Sacred Expedition" to work on the mission ranchos, developing trade in hides, agriculture and mineral extraction. Winding through productive fields surrounding new subdivisions grown up around earlier settlements, travelers in the 21st century call the highway 101. That morning, vineyards draped across the rolling hills were golden against a cumulous Fall sky.

Still Dreaming California

"Wine is the new California gold..." Regina mused aloud, interrupted as a sudden flock of blackbirds distracted her gaze. Swooping over the highway to land on the tiled roof of the old Mission *San Miguel Arc'angel*, the birds quickly nestled into the mystery of a past reality.

Regina and Reggie knew that the mission had been established by Franciscans 200 years before. It was interesting historical information, but also personal. Reggie had attended Franciscan schools and ultimately some of his Brothers had lived in San Miguel during their Novitiate. For Regina, the mission touched on a formative relationship in her childhood. A close friend of her grandmother's with deep roots in early California, had grown up on a farm adjacent to the Franciscan mission of *San Carlos Borromeo de Carmelo* near Monterey, and the missions had become a lifetime fascination. Her stories of early California had even included historical connections to Junipero Serra, the Franciscan Padre who had brought Christianity to Nuevo California. Sparking lifelong curiosity about Mission history, they had been on a quest all their lives, ultimately leading them down the *Camino Real,* on the lookout for adventure, scenic points, and the source of legend.

"Wings of change..." she contemplated.

"...all searching for Redemption" her companion continued philosophically." From the early *Padres* in search of souls, to Snowbirds seeking shelter from the storms... and crazy traffic!" he had to add as a passing semi blew them onto the shoulder.

"*Santa Maria!* Help get us to the border!" Reggie was praying for more than a line in the sand. They were traveling The *Path,* back into the early days of *Antigua California* where the *Camino* seemingly wandered through the veil of earlier times.

First exploring *Baja California* with their young family in 1980, Reggie and Regina had taken their cabover camper on the ferry over the Sea of Cortez from *Mazatlan* to scout the recently paved highway up the *California* peninsula. Enchanted by the beauty, it had been a pivotal discovery leading to many more winter adventures through the desert scape of *Baja*.

Meditating further on the thin veneer of the present, they followed the highway past the historic mission. A fascinating rest stop along the highway, they had visited many times. It had remained active to that day as a Parish Church, but instead of the mission bounty of the old days, stinky oil rigs now dotted the hills nearby. As they approached *Paso Robles,* they couldn't help but notice how many oaks had disappeared to make way for creeping vineyards and Factory Outlet Stores.

" Will the footprints of the past continue to disappear under this colossus of mall expansion?" Regina demanded in desperation, not really expecting a response. After thirty-five years of marriage though, Reggie instinctively understood what his partner was asking. Switching off the Country Western station they had been listening to, he replaced its noxious demand of "Shop 'til you drop!" - with some better messaging.

"Let's start getting into a Mexican frame of mind" he suggested, slipping in a favorite disk. The miles melted under Carlos Santana's sizzling riffs.

Pulling in behind a hotel/restaurant complex just beyond the old mission walls in *San Juan Capistrano*, Reggie found a shady spot to rest amidst an abandoned grove of gnarly old citrus trees. Ms. Chief and Mr. Sniff exuberantly bolted from the van. After numerous journeys along the *Camino Real*, the furry companions understood the need to take full advantage of pit stops. A survey of the area made it evident that not an extensive mission community had been overwhelmed by the new reality. An old *casita* in the orchard was almost hidden by a thick grouping of *bougainvillea* and instead of a reserve of water the *pila* was filled with garbage.

"Wow, I wonder if Father Serra planted any of these trees?" Regina fantasized, sentimentally referencing the iconic Father of California.

This prospect led to further investigation, while Reggie filled her in with an historical dissertation that included the information that the native converts had actually provided the forced labor that built the Mission Empire.

"Hey, we're talking Conquest here" Reggie reminded his traveling partner, then softening his tone, added, "Anyway, planting an orchard was probably preferable to annihilation."

Turning a corner, they discovered a tour bus delivering a modern horde of pilgrims to the entrance of the historical edifice. Joining the visitors to slip back a few centuries, Regina paused to read an inscription over the entrance.

"In God we trust.... Established in 1776". At the same time that the Declaration of Independence was being signed, the invasion of another indigenous people had begun in the Far West.

The twenty-first century border that divided California in 1848 defines that *Antigua California* developed by the Jesuit and Dominican missionaries and the *Nueva California* expanded north by the Franciscans during the Sacred Expedition. Tijuana's un-escapable jumble of political and economic blight blurs the reality that the border originally lay much further south, where *hectares* of crooked sticks run in rows up sandy hillsides, sheltering young plants under stretched plastic and tented greenhouse gardens make sure that winter tomatoes and strawberries will always be available at American markets.

The Scenic Highway and the toll-free road from the border converge in Ensenada. The main port for *Baja California* and the hub of trade for the modern *galleons*, it is there that the extracted products of Mexico are transported across the Pacific in exchange for manufactured products made in Asia, making the city a colossus of corporate shopping opportunity, as well as a profusion of Mexican arts and crafts. If visa arrangements haven't been dealt with at the border, this is where that has to happen. A mountainous red, white and green flag emblazoned by Mexico's iconic eagle with a snake, billows over the plaza where the immigration office deals with the paperwork reminding *gringos*, that this part of *California* belongs to Mexico.

Looking around from the plaza, Reggie and Regina could see that Ensenada still had quaint Mexican charm, with horse drawn carriages lined up to take visitors on tours through the old city. Regina had her picture taken with a burro spray painted like a zebra. The competing chorus of waterfront *taco* stands make it impossible to resist a snack, whatever time of day. Fun, but after following obscure road signs winding through the NAFTA maze of commercial enterprise, it was a relief to put Ensenada behind them.

Steep granite canyons lined with *California* sycamores follow the route of the missionaries, continuing south from Ensenada and eventually opening onto the broad fertile valley of *Santo Tomas*. Gnarly old grape vines and extensive remnants of olive orchards remind travelers that this was once a thriving mission area, supplying *Californians* with olive oil and alter wine.

A series of agricultural communities continue past *Santo Tomas*, home to a swelling population of immigrants. From one revolution to another, new settlers from Central America had begun to outnumber the indigenous peoples in providing the cheap labor necessary for modern factory farms. Historically, these supply settlements provided for travelers along the *Camino*

Real, either southbound for *Antigua California* or northbound to *Nueva California*. Between the border and *El Rosario*, messy graffiti identifies the electrical substations that fuel the revolutionary miracle of refrigeration that makes it all possible. A frustrating system of velocity *reductors* known locally as *topes*, protect the local population of pedestrians and stray dogs from the overwhelming stream of traffic, farm equipment and commerce along the congested, potholed highway. The sight of the spectacular Pacific coastline approaching *San Quintin* is a welcome sight for any traveler. It is here that the factory farms are left behind and the open spaces of wild *Baja California* begin.

"Which way now?" demanded Reggie, sliding to a stop on the edge of yet another monster swamp, spread across the muddy *camino*.

"We do have 4-wheel drive...." reminded Regina with just a hint of ambivalence, longingly eyeballing the distant sand dunes beginning to fade into a brilliant sunset.

"I don't think so" Reggie erupted, abruptly swerving their mud-caked vehicle toward yet another swampy track. They had gotten stuck before and he wasn't ready to chance the unknown depth of quicksand lying in wait for gullible victims. The next mud pit didn't seem quite as formidable and after a few more turns into the encroaching twilight, they at last pulled into the narrow driveway of their destination. It was about to become a fateful turning point in their journey.

Hotel Cielito Lindo, was a sweet little secret nestled along the Pacific coast, on the south end of the enterprising farming community of *San Quintin*. There was just enough time to take the dogs for a walk on the vast rolling sand dunes resting under the horizon of the fading sunset.

A very happy face new moon was just sliding into the Pacific as the travelers pushed into the *cantina* for a brew. Greeted by Mariachi music, a warm fire blazed behind them as they surveyed the scene of travelers and locals perched around the bar discussing the days catch over frosty Coronas while the waiter brought out heaping plates of steamed crabs.

"This looks like the spot" they agreed, signaling the bar tender while they slipped onto well-worn stools as a familial greeting welcomed them from the dance floor.

"Noooort!" It was their joust-about friend from the Faire, C.Nic Point. Wherever they went, they would always find a Scenic Point.

"It's always good to see you Nic, especially over a cold cerveza." The medieval knight charging from the front of Nic's t-shirt was bleeding a little *salsa casera*, but they hugged him anyway.

"I thought you'd be fast and furious in the studio" he quizzed them. "With the Renaissance Faire scheduled to open in mid-April, I expected you'd be getting ready." Nic's long hair flung a hint of residual glitter as he danced in place.

"Hey, no *problema*, we're taking some time for research and development." Reggie wasn't really in the mood for an interrogation just then. With the warm fire at his back, he was ready to mellow out.

"We always find so much inspiration here in the *Baja*." Regina was surprised that she had to remind Nic of their proverbial quest for the creative spirit. "So, *que onda*? What brings you to the *Baja*, Nic?"

"I'm on a mission of mercy. That's my nephew over there" he explained, pointing to a corner booth where a slumped figure was posed before a squadron of empty *Pacifico* bottles. His day glow jacket and matching baseball cap left no doubt that he smoked *Winstons.*

"He's been sucked dry by corporate management and is deeply in need of some quality R&R. You arrived just in time!" he confided. "We're on our way to *Bahia de Los Angeles* for some fishing and we're hauling his luxury panga with all its bells and whistles. I'm still trying to break my Dad's record - a 38 lb. Yellowtail! Of course, if we can snag a few sea bass dinners, all the better. Come with us." Licking his lips in anticipation, Nic led them over to meet Panga Buddy just as plates of spicy crabs and colder *cerveza* arrived. What could have been more perfect?

Turning inland toward *El Rosario*, the little caravan made a pit stop for an early breakfast. *Mama Espinosa's* restaurant on the edge of town, just past the PEMEX station, offers modern highway hospitality, good coffee and the best *Huevos Rancheros* along the *Camino Real,* as well as guide books, maps and curios, making Mama's a perfect opportunity to fuel up before the long stretch to *Bahia de Los Angeles.* Climbing into mountains with broad ridges and wide scenic vistas, it is always a relief to leave behind the crowded Pacific corridor and realize that there is still a lot of space in *California.* Pausing at the crest of the hill above the river valley of canyons strung east from *El Rosario* like beads on a rosary, they paused to reflect.

"It's probably for the best that *California* was divided the way it was" Reggie mused to Regina as they scanned the panoramic vista of unspoiled desert scape. "I shudder to imagine the level of exploitation that would have happened by now if the U.S. had been in control!"

The *Sonoran* desert vegetation begins after crossing the *Rio del Rosario.* Century plants and cordon cactus are reminders that this part of *Baja California* has a archetypal desert that includes a wide range of desert plants. A strong wind off of the Pacific was sweeping across the mountains while the little caravan wove erratically up and down the narrow highway, dodging a plethora of potholes as they headed south toward the intersection where they would be turning east toward the Sea of Cortez. As they passed through some of the most pristine desert areas on earth, they noticed a beer can being carelessly tossed from Panga Buddy's rig.

"Nic is right! This is definitely a case for emergency intervention. But that boy is a two-week project, at least" Regina declared hopelessly.

They were still contemplating the challenge when Reggie was forced to suddenly veer off the road in order to miss colliding with an air bourn deer! Flung completely over the rig they were following, it was wide eyed, bracing itself for landing as it bounced from the careening *panga.* Miraculously the deer was able to jump off and run away as Panga Buddy pulled over to evaluate the situation.

The desert that surrounded them was posed vigilantly along the rutted pavement as it wound into the *Sierra San Borja* Desert in a deceptively soft palette of sage and rose. But in reality, it was a vista of spikes and thorns that demanded respect for its honest attempt at survival. Curious buzzards started to circle as Regina seized upon a photo-op, posing Reggie in front of a giant twisted *Cordon* for a snapshot.

"Reggie, stop jumping around so much" she demanded, even while he was yanking a huge thorn from the sole of his new *zapatos,* shoes that he had recently purchased in Tijuana.

"Let's *vamos a la Bahia*" Reggie complained, limping back toward the van, suddenly anxious to resume the journey. "Shoot yourself why don't you!"

"*Por favor,* my darling, please help me carry this amazing boulder of quartz. I need it for a souvenir" she pleaded hopefully, prying at the monolithic specimen she'd been standing on.

Reggie looked back unsympathetically, even when he saw his *esposa* prick her butt on a spiny *chola*, revving up the engine for more impact even though Nic Point and his nephew were still checking their rig for front end damage.

They might have then missed an interesting historic point, except it was impossible to miss a handsome *caballero* on a brilliant white stallion in full *rancho* regalia, polished black leather, spurs and chaps, cantering alongside the *camino*. Having paused to offer assistance, he was now galloping his stallion onto a dirt road leading west, when they noticed a very small and rusty sign announcing an obscure turn off; Mission *San Fernando* - 4 km.

Reggie and Regina immediately put aside their ridiculous bickering to open their guidebooks. Seeing that Nic and his nephew were just then cracking cold *cervezas* to help with the inspection, it looked like there was time for a little exploration.

Turning onto the narrow gravel road, they caught up with the handsome *caballero* dismounting in the small *corral* of an old *rancho*. With the authority of local knowledge, he directed them further up the road that led to *San Fernando de Velicata* and areas of historical significance beyond the old mission. The tracks became increasingly concealed by overgrown vegetation, but eventually opened up onto a deserted valley when they reached the ruins.

Reading from their guidebook, Reggie filled in a little history. Established during the Spanish Expedition of Conquest, this was Junipero Serra's first mission. Originally home to a thousand natives, according to Dominican records, by the turn of the Century epidemics had reduced the native population to 360.

"In 1748, silver mining started south of San Antonio in the rugged mountain terrain at a place called Santa Ana, the site of one of the most important meetings in the history of the American West."

"Are you referring to the Sacred Expedition?" Regina interrupted, sensing a quantum clue to their own expedition.

Anxious to elaborate, Reggie continued reading. The information seemed to touch on the core of their own personal quest.

"In 1768, Viceroy Jose de Galvez, the personal representative of the King of Spain, made Santa Ana his headquarters. From there he sent for Junipero Serra, the newly arrived head of the Franciscan missionaries, and at that most unlikely of places they drew up the plans for the expedition that resulted a year later in the founding of his first mission in California."

"Santa Ana. That is a mighty fine nugget, *Señor."*

"Mission San Fernando Rey de Espana de Velicata was the first Franciscan mission, established in 1769 in the Indian area called Velicata, by Padre Presidente Junipero Serra. It was here that Serra's party had joined up with Governor Gaspar de Portola and his historic overland expedition of conquest, The Sacred Expedition, and the beginning of the Nuevo California chain of missions."

Imagining Governor Portola and Friar Serra meeting at this remote site during the Sacred Expedition, convening the parties of soldiers, native neophytes, herds and pack animals loaded with supplies, preparing for the departure to *San Diego, Velicata* had been the beginning of a *Nuevo California* chain of missions along an extended *El Camino Real.*

"Of course, Portola would have wanted to control this strategic area" Reggie cynically concluded. The green valley stretching before them, winding west to the Pacific between formidable desert hills, offered needed water and pasturage along the *Camino Real.*

"And *anxious for souls,* I can understand why Serra would found his first mission here." Regina was wondering how Serra had convinced the early converts to relinquish their lifestyle.

Under Franciscan direction the natives had developed a system of aqueducts, eventually supplying crops of wheat, corn and barley, providing an important supply station for future missions along the *Camino Real.* Looking out over the valley, new vegetation had all but obscured those ambitious efforts, leaving only a faint design over a reclaimed landscape.

"Now here we are, almost two and a half centuries later at the ruins of the very first of the new mission chain." After examining the eroded remains of adobe walls, they were curious to explore further.

Following the dogs along a dry aqueduct running below the cliff, Reggie and Regina were led into a narrowing rock gully with steep cliffs covered with petroglyphs; messages from generations of indigenous peoples living in that place for centuries before the diseases of conquest annihilated them. Geometric patterns chipped out of the sheer varnished walls depicted images of animals, information about the hunt, community, conflict and friendship. These were the stories of a people living with respect for the natural world.

Returning to the ruins of the Mission with a different perspective, they stared out over the valley.

"We're walking on the footsteps of Conquest, Reggie. Franciscan missions began here. How could a *sacred* expedition have gone so wrong?"

Spotting movement behind a towering cactus in the distance, **"How many trinkets did you get for this land?"** Reggie shouted out to the ancestors, with only echoes returning his call. Even after a Franciscan education, he was challenged to imagine any defense that could rationalize extinction of an indigenous people.

It was a question that remained unanswered as the 21st Century travelers returned to their own journey. A mighty endeavor had begun there at *Velicata* and all that was left of the dream was a few portions of eroded wall and mounds of crumbling adobe.

Punta Don Juan

Reggie and Regina were blissed out on the sand watching C.Nic Point and his nephew preparing their stateside luxury cruiser for launch. Huddled under a bright new turquoise Bimini, they were sorting through their gear and packing down the ice in their bait coolers while further down the beach pelicans rose from their perches to swarm fishermen pulling in with their catches, competing to scoop up the entrails as they were tossed from the boats. Overhead, aggressive seagulls were snatching the airborne morsels before they even hit the ground.

"Elephantes!"
Wispy cloud strands were stretching beyond the mountain tops as white caps began forming along the beach in front of their *Puerto Los Angeles casita.*

"High cirrus clouds with long curved filaments turned up at the end like an elephant's trunk usually forecast high winds" Nic had lectured them earlier, however his nephew hadn't paid any attention. Photos of proud fishermen posted over the bait freezer in the harbor store was all Buddy needed to know. Fondling a slippery bag of pink squid, he could only dream of launching his fishing Safari in the morning.

Equipped with dual Johnson 250's, he had promised them the cruise of their lives, only first he had to share all of his latest gadgets, bells and whistles with the locals, suspending them in bewilderment as each merchandising miracle was unveiled and inspected.

"Check out this rod! It telescopes from 3 to 8 feet in a jiffy and this reel is designed to handle a drag of 100 pounds! Hey, and check out these hootchies." Accustomed to live bait, the local fishermen seemed a bit skeptical about his brightly colored metal and plastic decoys.

Digging into a huge Walgreen shopping bag, Buddy began dispersing corporate advertising perks to the surprised fishermen who were soon decked out in Joe Camel t-shirts and Winston baseball caps.

"El Capitan es muy loco!" He was already making friends with the L.A. fishing community.

"Hey! Tomorrow we can drink our brew from these neoprene bottle insulators" and "here Reggie, I brought some extra lighters. So how about digging into your stash for a fatty later?"

Handing over a Marlboro brand lighter to his new mate, the *Capitan* continued rummaging through his magic bag and soon Regina was festooned in a bright florescent pink cap advertising *Gatorade*. Lighting up yet another cigarette, he stepped back approvingly.

"We're ready for the big one now" he exhaled emphatically, inviting his new *amigos* for a walk along the bay while Nic stayed to cook up a bag of halibut fillets that his nephew had traded for a *Joe Camel* blazer.

"I take care of the boat, but Uncle Nic does the cooking" he explained, fishing a bottle of *Tequila* out of his pocket and tossing his glowing butt into the sand.

Regina gave him a stink eye while she scooped up the offending butt. "Birds peck these up and get them stuck in their stomachs" she lectured him, while he blissfully charged away.

"Hey, let's just get fucked up." Leading the way up the beach, he passed the *tequila* to Reggie.

Mercifully Regina didn't push the point, but only because the strength of the wind suddenly made it hard to speak. Howling off of the desert with a vengeance, they were luckily able to find shelter beneath one of the beached *pangas* clustered together on the windswept shoreline.

"So, isn't it about 4:20? What about that fatty?" their Panga Buddy jokingly demanded, tossing another lighter at Reggie and sucking down a long hit of *tequila*.

Trapped by the elements, the intimacy of the overturned *panga* soon created a bond that was an invitation for soul searching. The wind was blasting the sand horizontal across the beach while they huddled together against the elements and within fifteen minutes Buddy had achieved his goal; he was definitely fucked up.

"I started to work for the corporation when I first got out of high school, but it was just something I was doing to make ends meet until I figured out what I really wanted to do." Interrupting his own thought for another hit of *tequila*, it was a while before the story was continued.

"I'm starting to think that maybe I'm missing it though." Long pause. "I mean... what I really want to do..." Another long pause. "It's just that the perks are so good with the corporation" he finished lamely.

"It can't be just about the perks Buddy!" Reggie was being direct. "It's gotta be about respect, too. Do you think they really care about you personally?"

It was just a minute before Buddy started to cry, his lament harmonizing with the deep howl of the wind blowing down from the pass as he sobbed piteously.

"I ...don't... have a life...sob... anymore. I'm salaried, so I can never say no to extra hours... I work all the time... and now my girlfriend left me... sob... I think she got tired of getting stood up all the time."

With this last confession, Buddy drained the last of the *tequila* and just sort of did a slow-motion slide into the sand, full surrender, staring up at his companions helplessly.

"It's pretty obvious that we've found the chink in his time warp continuum..." Reggie conferred with Regina philosophically.

"And I think it may be time for that emergency intervention that your Uncle was talking about. Pull yourself together Buddy" Regina encouraged, passing over her bottle of water. "Do you have a Plan B?" It was a while before she got any response.

In a whisper that they could barely catch above the wind, "Uncle Nic thinks I should start doing the Renaissance Faire."

All things considered, that sounded like a sensible alternative to Reggie and Regina.

The fishing Safari departed port before dawn. Gliding across water as smooth as glass into the *Canal de las Ballenas,* they rounded *Punta Don Juan* just in time to greet the rainbow light of daybreak reflected onto one hundred and eighty degrees of abalone sky. The *Capitan* had described a scenic tour exploring the coastline with a little trolling, but they hadn't expected such a day glow beginning of their big adventure.

"*Mire!* Who's that?" Regina was pointing toward the silhouette of a figure urgently gesturing towards them from the far side of a narrow slit at the base of the vertical cliffs just past the point, standing out against the rising sun.

"What an entrance! Must be Don Juan himself" joked *Capitan,* sarcastically referencing one of Regina's favorite literary icons, Don Juan Mateos, immortalized by Carlos Castenada in his books describing *"A Yaqui Way of Knowledge".*

"He probably wants to sell us a condo at the deserted development down the coast. They spent millions and now it just gets visited by the seals!"

"It looks more urgent." Regina wasn't appreciating their *Capitan's* sarcastic humor. Still concerned, "Shouldn't we at least get a little closer to check it out?" she continued. "Maybe he's stranded and needs help."

But Regina's curiosity about Don Juan was over-ridden by the appearance of a sleek fin whale, spouting just off the prow.

"Thar she blows" called out the *Capitan* gleefully as the gigantic form surfaced, breaking through the brilliant sunrise reflection so close that the blow had them all dripping. Turning toward the giant creature as it slid back into the depths, *Capitan* turned on the electric depth finder to follow the huge form below them, ignoring Regina's weak protest as the waving figure faded in importance. Only Nic noticed the sudden appearance of a giant eagle ascending the pinnacle of the majestic point.

"She might be down for a while..." *Capitan* explained. "She's heading south, so let's follow her for a while and then we'll keep heading on to the tip of *Coronado* for some fishing."

Continuing his monologue as they sliced through a sea as smooth as mercury. "I know that Fin Whales are capable of submergence for up to twenty minutes..."

Miles down the coast they were immersed in wonderment, following along towering coastal cliffs infused with geological history and a shoreline rich with wildlife. According to C.Nic Point, of the two hundred and sixty species of birds in *Baja California*, two hundred and fifty-nine of them could be found in the archipelago surrounding Los *Angeles*.

Multitudes of pelicans starred at them suspiciously from rocky perches, while gulls helicoptered over them curiously for signs of entrails. Spotting a family of Blue Footed Boobies roosting mid-way up a sheer cliff, Uncle Nic had coaxed his nephew in for a closer look, when Regina noticed something out of place. An unfortunate creature was hanging perilously close to the edge of oblivion, stranded on a rock and tightly shackled by netting that it evidently hadn't been able to loosen for some time. The seal was so weak that it could raise its head for only a second in response to Regina's sympathetic greeting.

"Nort! Nort!" she called out hopefully. "We have to help it" she pleaded tearfully, ignoring the barely submerged rocks surrounding the helpless victim.

"I can't jeopardize my boat, plus I don't want to get bitten." The *Capitan* stubbornly refused to intervene.

"This is probably a job for Alfredo's Animal Rescue" Nic suggested sympathetically. "We'll give him the location of the seal as soon as we return" he promised, but it was a sad departure as they all realized how pollution was affecting the environment of wildlife. The pristine waters explored and described by John Steinbeck in his "Log from the Sea of Cortez" as recently as the 1930's was now suffering fatal challenges.

But it was impossible to dwell on the hardships of the natural world as the craggy coastline of magical wonderment continued to reveal a treasure of wildlife. Overhead, an osprey was returning to its nest with a Brants duck hanging from its talons, lunch for the hungry chicks peering out from a driftwood nest perched on a ledge far above.

"Hey, check out that boil down the coast!"

Determined to get back to fishing, *Capitan* soon had his super modified slicing through the water toward the commotion. A large school of *Pargo* were being corralled into a tight knot, churning up the surface in their frenzied attempt to survive. Racing toward the spectacle, they weren't the only ones hoping to get lucky. Gulls and Albatros were heading in from every direction to circle the turmoil and as they got closer, they could see why.

"Dolphins!"

Breaking off from the pod, a squadron of the sleek animals were bounding toward them in gleeful greeting.

"Let's give 'em a thrill!"

Pushing down on the throttle, *Capitan* soon took them to eight knots with the dolphins racing alongside, spinning at the helm, veering back and forth in front of them in competition for the lead position then rolling away to be replaced by a *compadre*, with yet another group replacing them as they tired.

"Nort, nooooort!" The high-pitched version of her tribal greeting seemed to attract the creatures while Regina leaned over the side of the boat in an attempt to communicate with the mystical beings. Straining to reach out to them, she was close enough to recognize various markings and there were a few individuals that were very persistent, but eventually they returned to fishing, leaving the *Safari* to their own fishing.

"When we reach *Punta Soledad*," Nic explained, pointing toward a monolithic formation looming several miles further down the rocky coast, "we'll have reached *Bahia de Las Animas*... the Bay of Spirits."

Seeing activity on the depth finder, *Capitan* slowed down. Setting their poles in high anticipation, he and his crew were soon busy hauling in Sierra as they leisurely trolled south toward the cape. Of course there were numerable species that were caught and released, but they soon had their cooler filled with Sierra, Sea Bass and a couple of nice Yellowtails, although none big enough to break the record set by Nic's Dad.

"Guess I have to leave something to look forward to" he lamented cryptically.

Sipping brews and munching on the remains of last night's dinner, *Creedence Clearwater Revival* was spiraling into the ether when they rounded the point into the Bay of Spirits. Right away it felt weird.

Laying below a vast ramp of sand, an abandoned beach resort blindly stared out at them from vacant windows and darkened doorways, but as they trolled closer for a better look, they saw that it wasn't really deserted after all. A community of seals began streaming out of the ghostly buildings to greet the *gringos*, plunging into the water to get a closer look at the intruding panga which was soon surrounded by the wildly barking creatures.

"*Sacramento!* What a reception." And as if that wasn't strange enough, Regina proceeded to reel a four-foot octopus into the boat.

The poor creature was visibly terrified, scrambling around the crowded deck looking for a place to hide, while the humans pretty much did the same.

"I want to release him!" Regina exhorted fiercely.

Wrestling to remove the hook from the beak of the venomous cephalopod, Nic became a tangle of tentacles until he was finally able to throw the creature overboard, where they watched it disappear into a spreading cloud of ink. The darkness even seemed to be encompassing the boat as they were abruptly thrown into shadow. Turning their eyes to the sky, a heavy row of *Elephantes* were crossing the sun and they could hear the call of the wind as it menacingly swooped over the horizon from the Pacific. Whipping up a distinct wind line on the Sea, a turbulent zone of white caps was bearing down on them like a crazed herd of elephants. The seals and gulls were racing back to their resort as *Capitan* and crew realized how far south, they had explored on their little safari.

"Maybe we should wait out the storm with the seals" Regina suggested hopefully, but their captain was undeterred by their impending fate.

"Hey, we're almost out of beer!"

That explained everything as far as *Capitan* was concerned and their fantasy fish safari slipped into history as they tightened up their life jackets, tied down the gear and prepared themselves for a rough ride back to port. Towering above them, the approaching squall was becoming a menacing monster, churning up the darkened sea like an agitating washing machine, whipping up a purple haze that was quickly obliterating visibility along with any preconceived sense of invincibility.

Following the rugged coastline that had seemed so magical just a little earlier, now had become a nightmare of hidden rocks and sudden wild currents with the Safari and her crew straining to stay on course. Forced to remove the Bimini and with waves coming at them in every direction, they were soon dripping wet. Regina was struggling to tighten her swivel chair as Reggie lurched to help her, almost falling overboard.

"I'd suggest mutiny" joked Regina, shouting out over the melee, "but I don't think that would improve the situation."

"*Santa Maria!*" Reggie shouted, dragging himself toward the relative safety of his chair. "There's no getting off this bus, so..." he trailed off, "...we better enjoy the ride!" Shifting his attention to the challenge of roping himself to the chair, Reggie was being realistic.

Resolutely hunkering down with the captain steady at the wheel, keeping their prow above water most of the time while draining the last of the *cerveza*, "just for courage", it seemed to be working as they inched their way along the coastline, every mile a little victory until by dusk they had almost reached L.A. Bay.

When they again saw *Don Juan* he was almost obscured in the fading evening light. He was gesturing more urgently than before, this time flashing a spotlight that got their attention. Piercing through the gathering darkness, they watched long enough to recognize an SOS signal.

"Is there anything that we're missing here?" *Capitan* quizzed, looking around to suddenly see a sheer wall of water racing toward them at a speed that would absolutely make it impossible for them to reach the safety of the *Bahia*.

"What the...?"

Capitan was stunned, but the question was left hanging as Nic Point abruptly hit his nephew on his back between his shoulders, a *Don Juan* move enabling him to take control of the vessel without a struggle. Steering the cruiser in a confident arc that placed the ominous wave behind them, Nic navigated a trajectory in line with the pulsing signal from *Don Juan*, a beam which now seemed to reach out and connect them with the *Nagual*.

"Let's all be warriors!" Nic shouted out to his mates with immaculate intention. Now that the sheer wall of water was rapidly gaining on them, were the doubters finally ready to take a chance on the fabled Sorcerer?

The Safari was jetting into the unknown, when they saw the keyhole. Just behind the point, almost obscured by deepening twilight, the appearance of that narrow gap gave them something to believe in. The giant face of the wave was gaining on them as Nic angled the panga to catch the momentum, pumping just enough power from the awesome JOHNSONS to match the surge and with a mighty leap of intention they launched into heightened awareness, catching the wave, surfing straight into the mystery, death just over their shoulder, surrounded by eternity, something beyond their understanding swept them onto the path with heart.

Still Dreaming California

The faint glow of dawn was filtering through the narrow entrance onto their feeble reality as they awakened together from what seemed like a dream. No sign of *Don Juan*, but finding themselves straddling a rocky crag precariously hanging 25 feet above the water line absolutely stopped their world. The last thing they could collectively remember was a cascade of water, a luminous bubble opening to surround them and the shrill call of an eagle as they hurtled into the void. The rest was sheer mystery.

"Ha! Ha, haaaa!" Their peak experience had become a crossroad, an intersection of two worlds perched on the edge of time. An echo mounted as Buddy erupted with laughter.

"Ha..a..aa…aaa..aaaaaa…" The sudden awareness of paradox was changing him.

It wasn't with feelings of grief or loss that he surveyed the wrecked shell of his boat, rather it was the knowledge that they were all still alive that imputed a sense of pure joy. By the time Buddy had mounted the prow of his former super modified and spread his new wings of perception to greet the world, they were all helplessly howling with laughter.

"Ha, haa…haaa…aaa!" and "Eeeeeeoow!" and "Nooooooorrrrrrt!"

The echoes of triumph bouncing off of sheer stone walls were what welcomed the dawn arrival of the search party, who probably thought the shipwrecked sailors were all hysterical.

"This is what freedom looks like" C.Nic Point called down to the astounded rescuers gathering below their craggy perch.

"Freedom! Freeeee,,,dom… freeeed…ooommmm…."

Buddy decided to abandon his *panga*, hopelessly wedged in the rock anyway, as a tribute to the *Nagual*.

"Actually, the decision was way beyond his power" Nic suggested to Reggie and Regina, shaking his head dubiously. "The *Nagual* actually left him no other choice."

The crew of the Safari was keeping a low profile on the side of the crowd gathered around his now legendary nephew.

"Well yeah" Reggie agreed. "I don't think the hull of the *Safari* is good for anything else but legend now, anyway."

The transformation of the former *Capitan* was almost complete as he humbly described the miracle of their survival to the local fisherman, the sudden arrival of the giant sheer wall, the appearance of a mysterious *Don Juan* character and their magical escape from mortal danger. He even went on to briefly describe a new future for himself, free of corporate domination.

"Even though it means giving up all the corporate perks" he cryptically explained to the perplexed fishermen.

"I'm taking my uncle's advice" he revealed to his mates as they were preparing for departure. "I'm thinking about a line of essential oils at the Renaissance Faire. I have connections through the Corporation that'll help me get started. Then maybe a trip to Nepal to develop a source for incense …"

"That's amazing Buddy. Sounds like we'll be seeing more of you at the Faire." Regina was luminous as she posed her new *amigo* for a photo with his uncle. A radiant smile of satisfaction spread out over Nic's face as he realized the new bonds that had developed for his nephew during their pivotal adventure.

While Buddy was planning a new life, Reggie and Regina had reached their own crossroad. Time to head back to the studio. Their contacts with the natural world and their fleeting glimpse of the *Nagual* had given them a lot of inspiration.

"*Don Juan* has blessed us with a Renaissance of spirit." They were already sketching out new designs of whales, pelicans, octopus and fish that would soon enhance their work at the Faire.

Pausing to pose for Buddy while he took one last snap, Reggie somehow managed to close the van door on a dog tail.

"Hey, no whining! You dogs have a lot to be thankful for. You're just lucky not to be spending the rest of your lives scrounging the beach for fish heads!"

"Adios amigos. Hasta la vista!"

Under a crisp desert sky, the soaring call of an eagle was a fleeting reminder of the mystery they had shared.

A Moment in San Ignacio

It had been a long stretch from breakfast in Catavina as a small caravan pulled into shady spaces on the plaza across from the old mission. Reggie and Regina weren't about to let that particular scenic point slip past without at least a cursory introduction. Their traveling companions were newcomers to Baja California and the beautiful date-palm oasis of San Ignacio was a jewel of the desert not to be overlooked. After making the parched crossing from Guerrero Negro, the lush spring fed ponds were like heaven to the travelers, just as it must have seemed to the early missionaries.

"Could any of them have imagined a future of air-conditioned exploration along a now paved *El Camino Real?*" Regina reflected pointlessly over her walkie-talkie.

Running through the *Vizcaino Biosphere Reserve* to the *San Ignacio Lagoon* opening onto the Pacific, it had since become a World Heritage site, a protected wildlife sanctuary for gray whales and four species of endangered sea turtles.

It was *siesta* time as they checked out the sleepy *plaza,* but they imagined that curious eyes were most likely inspecting them from ancient doorways as they pried themselves from tightly packed vehicles. Even though Surfer Steve was on a single-minded safari for fish and surf, he was soon leading the way across the cobbled street and up well-worn stairs to stand in awe before the weathered, carved doorway of one of the original *California* missions. Begun in 1728, a stoic monument to *San Ignatio's* historical importance along the *Camino Real,* the Moorish style stone facade, festooned with the crest of a Spanish King and guarded by angels, audaciously loomed above them.

"Imagine the impact such an edifice must have had on the aboriginal inhabitants." Always keen for architecture, Fern was gazing straight up a quilt of stone while her compadres irreverently stepped around her to enter the cool interior of history where a scary stone face greeted them from above a fount of holy water. Gradually adjusting to the dim light, they were irresistibly lured towards a gold rimed altarpiece smoldering from the shadows at the far end of the transept. The vaulted ceiling above the nave looked like it had been freshly painted. A well-worn aisle led to the alter. Probably carried by the invaders from New Spain, a statue of *Saint Ignacio* surrounded by angels, gazed out onto empty pews. A couple of nuns tended the alter below him, arranging flowers and conversing reverently.

Following the Stations of the Cross as they led to the alter, Regina watched Christ carry his Cross to Redemption... and then eventually further, across three seas to this distant desert.

"It was a heavy load" she thought to herself, "but He had help along the way." First the Order of Jesuits, then the Franciscans, followed by the Dominicans, had determinedly brought Christianity and Spanish culture to the impoverished people of *California* since 1683. Halfway down the aisle, sharp pillars of sunlight sliced through a doorway leading out onto a dusty courtyard where a few decrepit old cactus were all that remained of what had probably once been a productive garden. It had obviously been some time since it had been cared for.

Slipping into a well-worn pew beneath the gaze of the Saint, it seemed like a good place to pause and reflect on their own journey. Sliding her palm along the smoothness of the aged wooden pew, Regina first gave thanks that she could still kneel. She knew that the hours spent driving that day were going to make it hard to stand up when she finished her meditation.

She and Reggie were Snow-birds, fleeing damp winters for the deserts of *Baja California*, but the early missionaries had come to save souls. Imagining the early *Cochimi* people, she thought how mystified they must have been by the pomp of this new faith. Through their circumstance of poverty and with the conquering arm of Spain closing in around them, they had eventually been forced to believe in this pompous symbol of conquest and a promise of redemption.

"Jesus Saves... really? Too bad that their new religion couldn't save them from soldiers, smallpox, syphilis and plague" Regina contemplated sadly. According to historical arithmetic, when the Franciscans arrived to take over the missions from the Jesuits, the indigenous populations had already been greatly reduced through the diseases brought to the peninsula. An estimated 30,000 to 40,000 natives had by the Franciscan census of 1768, been reduced to 7140 Christianized natives - that were referred to as *neophytes*. In *San Ignatio,* that number soon became practically zero. New people had arrived to take up the faith, and two and a half centuries later, fresh flowers were still being placed at the feet of the Saints and the carved stone baptismal fount was worn smooth from the touch of the Saved.

Along with the blast of afternoon light as they emerged from historical reverie, the travelers were disoriented by the flashing lights of the local *Policia* driving at the head of a procession that rapidly filled up the plaza. Uncomfortable as obvious outsiders, they watched a shiny white pick-up pull in at the foot of the stairway, blocking their departure. Then there was a sensation of being frozen in time as they watched a tiny white coffin with ornate gold trim being lifted from the truck bed. Then they were enveloped by a wave of community mourning, a parallel reality where nobody seemed to notice them as the dead baby was carried past. The visitors exchanged awkward glances as they bowed their heads out of respect for the family, but while the last stragglers climbed the worn stone steps, the hollow glance of one young man briefly connected them to his reality, just a momentary glance before he dutifully followed his people to disappear through the towering doorway to salvation, but it was at least acknowledgement of their presence in his world.

The murmur of mass followed them down to the plaza, where *siesta* time was evidently over and doors were being flung open. Merchants appeared from darkened doorways to spread their wares onto the sidewalks with the colorful displays that make shopping in Mexico so entertaining.

"*Santa Maria, datiles!*" Reggie was ready to stock up on a local specialty, while his *compadres* situated themselves on a bench beneath a towering shade tree to order hot dogs from a steaming cart. They were all soon munching *comidas,* dripping salsas as they studied their maps.

"Through the volcanic region of *Très Virgines,* down into Hells Canyon and then to our first glimpse of the Sea of Cortez." Reggie coordinated the route they would be taking with mounting enthusiasm.

They were still contemplating gas and milage to *Mulege* when silence again returned to the plaza and the little coffin emerged from the church to lead a procession to the graveyard.

"Still following their path with heart" Fern murmured to her friends as the descendants solemnly walked together up the hill to join another little soul with the ancestors, leaving the travelers from *El Norte* to ponder their own path.

They were thoughtful as they returned to their vehicles. Folding up maps and tuning on their walkie-talkies, they circled back toward the *Camino Real,* driving slower this time and noticing things along the route that they had missed before; a *gringo* book store just off the plaza; scattered remnants of the rock wall engineered by the early *padres* and stacked by the local ancestors to contain the river; a hollowed donkey carcass swarming with insects.

"Too bad we didn't miss that!" Surfer Steve sarcastically radioed to his *compadres,* rolling up his windows against a sudden swarm of flies.

"Hey, we don't want to miss any scenic points" Reggie imperiously radioed back, pulling up onto the shoulder of the highway to pause for another brief powwow.

"There's always settlement around water here in Baja." That afternoon the pond below them was swarming with vacationing kayakers, sliding smoothly through the glassy reflection of sky.

Looking back at the dramatic afternoon light radiating from the palm oasis where they had just shared a brief episode, Regina snapped pictures from the van window. Knowing that such a magical connection couldn't be channeled simply through a photo, it could still be a personal reminder of that brief moment in *San Ignacio* when the shroud of the oasis had parted for the visitors and their illusion of separation had been pierced by a Scenic Point and the glimpse of a different destiny.

Mulege Heroico

The wind was fierce over the pueblo as Reggie and Regina coasted down a steep stretch of El Camino Real into Mulege. This was the place where invading Americans had been defeated in 1847 during the Mexican American War, and the vultures were still circling. Taking advantage of an afternoon *chubasco*, hundreds of the ominous creatures were spiraling in concentric columns over the historic oasis. Hypnotically drawn into the spectacle, Reggie and Regina were eventually led to the historic mission Santa Rosalia de Mulege.

Perched on a rocky knoll above the historic *pueblo,* the stoic stone citadel is the second oldest mission in *Baja California.* Established in 1705 by Jesuit missionaries, its wide *vistas* encompass both the river as it leads to the Sea of Cortez, and its vast palm estuary, fading into the mountainous western horizon.

Unlike the Mexican capitulations in *La Paz* and *San Jose del Cabo, Capitan* Manuel Pinada had made a courageous stand there in heroic *Mulege*, refusing an ultimatum from American forces in the Pacific Coast Campaign. As American citizens,

Reggie and Regina were entertained by the spectacle of the historic invasion; a small force of American sailors struggling up a steep village hillside covered in spiky cactus, under bombardment from indigenous sniper fire! With 100 militiamen in an insurgent ambush from the jungle estuary, the Mexicans had driven the occupying forces back to their ship by nightfall. The resistance had begun in *Mulege* and was the pivotal event that had alerted the Americans to the revolt developing since President Polk had declared the *California* territory property of the United States.

"I heard that there weren't really 100 militiamen, that they had collected every *sombrero* in the village and perched them on sticks to intimidate the invaders, heh, heh!" That human element of the scenario seemed hilarious to Reggie.

"The natural elements here, don't make invasions very easy" Regina sarcastically reminded him.

"Yeah, well look how many of us are here now. Don't underestimate the power of creativity" Reggie quipped back defensively, referring to the modern invasion of *gringos*. The paving of the *Camino Real* in the later part of the 20th century had unleashed a flood of migration for both business and pleasure.

Spreading west toward the *Sierras de Guadalupe,* the knoll was an awesome vantage point to experience a panoramic sunset, with a swirling sky-scape changing colors every minute. The bats and owls were abandoning their perches, as vultures and herons waited to take their places for the night shift. Far below, protected from the wind, a peaceful lagoon offered shelter to water fowl, and they could imagine, swarms of mosquitos. Somewhere from the village beyond the mission, guitar riffs from Carlos Santana were blasting out at mega-decibels over the oasis like a sacred mantra.

"What do you want ... what are you looking for?" Still wondering why, after three centuries.

The visitors and their dogs slid into reflection, while the wind seemingly carried the cosmic vibrations of Santana's steamy guitar riffs into the setting sun. Then with the brilliant golden orb settling into the dancing horizon, they were greeted unexpectedly by a familiar salutation.

" Noooort! I knew I'd find you here!" Appearing like an apparition from beneath the spiraling column of vultures, it was their illustrious friend from the Faire, C.Nic Point.

Sharing a group hug, the last spectacular rays of day fanned out into the gathering twilight. "Now we're really feeling the magic!"

"When I heard that you two had escaped south again for some R&R time I knew it was time. The relentless war news and propaganda in the States has been exhausting." Nic continued on with a tirade of grim current events that completely reinforced the wisdom of their current hiatus.

"Yeah, that's how we were feeling too" commiserated Reggie soberly. "So much 9-11 tragedy in the news.... It was a horrible event, but you know, on the same day 24,000 people starved to death on the planet. So, now it's the *March on Terror* and the quest to control mid-East oil reserves while the economy flounders, schools and hospitals are closing and our civil rights are being eroded."

"It's overwhelming" empathized Regina sadly. "We protest, we petition and we pray, and while imagination is more important now than ever, it's a challenge to get into the studio and focus. Down here in *Baja California*, the simplicity of survival always refreshes our creative spirit."

"And now the drumbeats toward war." Nic didn't sound even remotely optimistic. "Some things about American politics are so predictable."

The vultures were settled into their palm perches, replacing the night feeders as the gathering dusk and the strength of the wind evoked a moment of shared camaraderie with the natural world. Forced to abandon the horizon of jagged peaks and plateaus the travelers sought shelter in the protective womb of the oasis.

"Hey, what's the matter with your dog?" inquired the *Patron* with only a slight accent, kindly taking notice of Mr. Sniff, stretching stiffly and hobbling over to the nearest palm tree to relieve himself.

"He'll be okay. He's an old dog and it's been a long journey" explained a sympathetic Reggie, reaching over to grip the welcoming hand. "We're ready to settle for the night if you have a space available."

"I just had to ask, because I want to tell you about something that might help him. Clay water." Their host was serious as he persistently went on to describe some healing techniques that he claimed had been very successful for both man and beast. Evidently, the clay in the area had amazing healing qualities. Along with shark cartilage and local *medicinals*, it was all very convincing as he described many miracle cures that he had helped to facilitate.

Eventually they were directed toward a peaceful camping spot overlooking the river. The sky was still slightly purple as the line-up of pelicans along the river bank relocated to accommodate the campers. The weary travelers were ready for the cure, but clay water was not what they had in mind.

"Here's to health" they toasted, downing a shot of *tequila* while the dogs cautiously sampled the clay water.

The *gringos* were ready to settle into the shelter of the oasis, making arrangements for their stay when they met Judy, an expat from the States, at the *oficina*.

"It doesn't matter where I'm from, because I'm never going back!" she exclaimed with a laugh and a haughty toss of her head toward a small trailer nestled in a nearby grove of date palms.

"That trailer is home now. I crossed the border two years ago with a truck, a duffle bag of stuff and $20 in my pocket. I thought I was going to die here. I had cancer so bad, I had no other expectation. Before long I was broke and out of gas. I was parked at a Pemex station when a young Mexican farmer pulled up in a beat up little Celica."

"Ni-i-ice ri-i-ide, *Seniorita*."

"Well, I said, I'll trade it for your Celica and a full tank of gas."

"*Santa Maria!* Are you serious? Is it stolen? I told him it wasn't. I had the papers and everything, so he said he'd be right back. Well, I drove that Celica until it ran out of gas. I just pulled over to the side of the road, put up the hood and before long somebody stopped and helped me. That kept happening one gallon at a time. People were so kind, feeding me, letting me stay at their homes. Along the way, I got arrested and they took my papers. Before I got locked up, another prisoner gave me money and told me to just go. They'll never give you your papers again without a bigger bribe."

"When I got here I was so sick I couldn't go on any further. *El Patron* took me in and healed me with clay water and shark cartilage."

The three amigos stared incredulously at her healthy body with admiration for her faith and courage.

"So, what does your family back in the States think of your story?"

"They were my problem in the first place and I don't want to see them again" she confessed. "They don't need to know where I am. This is my family now."

Following her gesture toward the campground, they began to understand about Judy's new family, noticing that many of the campers at the campground were listlessly hanging around their rigs, realizing that they also might be on the clay water, shark cartilage diet recommended by *El Patron.*

"I'm glad the shark cartilage is helping these people" Nic reflected sympathetically, "but I know of a little *cantina* in town where they make the best *chili rellenos. Vamos a comer, amigos!*"

Reggie had been up since before dawn, trying to entice Regina to give up the comfort of her warm sleeping bag. They had stayed at the *cantina* for one-too-many *margaritas* the night before and even though an expedition to see cave paintings had sounded great at the time, now she was having second thoughts.

"Get up! Nic is already running the dogs down the river to the lighthouse for some exercise before a day at the end of their ropes. We want to be ready when the guide gets here to pick us up."

Reggie was holding a high premium on promptness that morning, but Regina was holding out for special treatment and

Reggie didn't let her down. Thick Mexican coffee, plus the promise of adventure in the canyons beyond the oasis actually got her up before the vultures that morning.

As Reggie had expected, their guide arrived promptly with the rising sun. Leaving the scavengers to spread their wings in the warmth of early morning, they climbed into a faded, late model van and headed out for adventure.

Salvador Drew had intense green eyes, which helped to explain his unlikely surname. A local Mexican who advertised his Adventure Tours in all the tourist spots of *Mulege,* had assembled a congenial group of tourists curious about the ancient peoples of the area. A gay anthropologist from Canada, two French biologists, a phycologist couple from Israel, Reggie and Regina and C.Nic Point headed out of town followed by the morning sun, while Salvador kept a running discourse on local history and desert life. His grandmother had been a local *Bruha,* a sorceress, and he was evidently continuing in the tradition.

"The leaves from that tree can be tucked into your sox to cure foot fungus and two drops from it's fruit cures constipation in ten minutes" he lectured while skipping west along a dusty washboard road that had Regina wondering if she might wet her pants.

"Don't ever touch that tree" Salvador emphasized, pointing to a scrawny specimen alongside the road. "It's extremely poisonous. Don't even stand under it!" That kind of information made all his clients really glad that they were with a local guide.

"This road eventually continues to the Pacific" Salvador explained to them as Bert from Vancouver released the chain unlocking the barbed wire and stick gateway to the massive 5000 *hectare Rancho Trinidad.* Curious cattle and burros loped out of the way as the equally curious tourists snapped their pictures. By then the road had narrowed to a rocky trail winding between giant blossoming *Cordon* cactus with the tour guide continuing his informative dialogue. Red tipped *Ocotio* were brilliant against the blue skies of morning and yellow *Palo Verde* dotted the desert scape like eye candy as they followed the trail into timeless solitude.

Approaching the foot of the mountains, they were headed toward a narrow canyon, opening seductively from sheer walls of colorful stone. Salvador parked under a boney tree near a muddy watering hole heavily scattered with cow pies and after passing around bottled water and simple snacks he began the walking tour into a canyon where the early *Cochimi* tribal people had spent their time during the hot parts of the year in cave shelters.

The explorers were soon embraced by an ancient reality. Hopping from rock to rock across a sliver of flowing water, they followed the canyon into narrowing stone walls. Groupings of palms had tenaciously managed to insert themselves amidst giant boulder piles, creating a miniature Eden protected from the perils of the '*poke ya, stick ya*' desert that they had left behind. As their eyes adjusted to the shadowy world, Salvador pointed out numerous caves that the tribal families had used for shelter. Leading them further up a steep incline and along a narrow ledge to the entrance of a major cave he paused for effect, allowing his clients to discover for themselves the reality of those early inhabitants.

Settling down on the cool sand in the cave, while their eyes adjusted to the dim light, they gazed in amazement as an ancient world slowly came into focus. Dancing energetically around them in hues of red, ochre, charcoal and white was a story shared through the creative spirit: Graceful images of wildlife and the hunt; lizards, rabbits and deer prancing and leaping across the ceiling in overlapping patterns, human stick figures in obvious pursuit, ready with their arrows and spears, while depictions of foxes, tortoise and coyotes sought refuge in the shadows. There were images of bounty from the sea, but seemingly they had been a culture without agriculture. The pattern of human hand prints dispersed among the animal imagery, witnessed the history of a long ago people, evidence of an animistic way of life imbedded in the fabric of life on Earth.

"I can easily imagine the stories told by the *shamans* around the campfire with all the spirits springing to life from these cave walls" Regina romantically fantasized. She was always looking for a good story.

"Is this really what Jesus saved them from?" muttered Reggie cynically. "Earth, water, wind and fire. These are stories from the natural world."

"This is the life that disappeared when Christians came to save them. Were they Saints, or were they Monsters?" With his own special sense of satire, Nic intuitively exposed the irony, while the echos of the ancestors asked the question over and over.

Bahia de Conception

Fluorescent cumulonimbus clouds skimmed the horizon of a colorful dawn as a line of Pelicans swooped along the glassy water of the *Bahia de Conception,* just beyond the listing hull of a very weathered ketch, tattered sails drooping from the mast, a faded suggestion of a smugglers wet dream.

"That Captain better get out here and get those pumps going" cautioned a stretching Reggie to nobody but the dogs. C.Nic Point was already out fishing and Regina was on vulture time again, waiting to spread her wings into the warmth of the rising sun.

"Did you say you were fixing coffee?" called a hopeful voice from inside the van.

By the time she emerged from her comfy sleeping bag after a cup-a, Reggie was off to collect a bucket of clams and the other campers along the beach were well on their way to a day of adventure out on the Bahia. Rigging up their various water-craft, they were all focused on creating new dreams. The recently widowed tugboat Captain from New Jersey was still trying to coax his young Labrador onto his shiny new aluminum boat. The newly retired fisherman from Alaska was already streaking toward the rising sun in his Hove-craft, quickly disappearing behind the cactus silhouette of a craggy point on his way to a day of fishing around the clusters of rocky islands. The couple from Toronto who had just lost their grown son to cancer, were settling into their kayaks, gliding quietly onto the glassy water. They had been sharing their stories through the camaraderie of nightly beach campfires. The challenge of maintaining a creative spirit in the face of disappointments, described them all. These foreigners had migrated to the beaches of *Baja* hoping for healing.

Heroico Mulege, the inspiration for the resistance during the Mexican American War of 1847, insuring that *Baja California* would remain Mexican, was now occupied by legions of migrant *gringos*, camped out on the beaches, creating a cluttered landscape of vans, campers trailers and tattered palm roofed *palapa* camps. Spread out over every meter of the majestic white shoreline, as close as they could edge their rigs to the high tide mark and still leave room for beach chairs.

"What a paradox that so much of *Baja's* most desirable real estate is now occupied territory." Regina pondered the anomaly, becoming fixated on the abandoned ketch, listing now in the light morning breeze.

Settling into a faded beach chair facing the sun, she slipped into a meditation on her own unfulfilled expectations and disappointments. Thankful for the respite that BCS offered from news and current events, she reached her arms to the sky, embracing a moment of healing before the untimely interruption of capitalism.

Parking behind the line up of campers, early-bird vendors were already honking for sales along the dusty playa. Hot *tamales*, groceries, water, beer and ice were delivered daily from nearby *Mulege* in coolers crammed into the beds of battered pick-ups. Entrepreneurial Mexicans were busily exploiting their opportunities as Reggie returned proudly with a bucket of clams. Knowing how good a fresh *boleo* loaf would taste later with clam chowder, he quickly continued over to the pick-ups to negotiate, leaving Regina to meditate on his catch.

Regina began to shed layers. Wondering if it was time to ask Reggie to lather her up with some Hawaiian Tropic, the conspicuous arrival of a weathered old Toyota wagon interrupted the solitude. Determinedly edging itself through a narrow passage between two oversized R.V.s to find a space under a corner of the *palapa* next to them, they stared curiously as a deeply tanned hippy chic wearing a tattered off the shoulder *Grateful Dead* t-shirt proceeded to unload no less than seventeen dogs and puppies of unlikely sizes and breeds, for some playtime on the beach. Of course Mr. Sniff and Ms. Chief got all excited about the invasion, starting a round of butt sniffing and posturing that was hard to ignore. Apologizing for the inconvenient interruption, the hippy chic proceeded to volunteer her story.

"Stray dogs have become a terrible problem here in the *Baja*." Conscientiously scooping up a fresh doggie pile and heaping it into a bag, she began to elaborate.

"Snowbirds come down for the winter with their dogs, and about the same time that they want to start home, their bitches are dropping pups. Not wanting to travel with a brood, they abandon them. I tried to find an agency that would deal with the strays that I was collecting, but there wasn't one. Finally I started getting them shots myself and going door to door to find them homes. That works with the pups, but it's hard to help the older dogs."

Reaching over to scoop up another fresh land mine, she added "I've already been banned from *Saticoy* and *Coyote* beaches, but

I know the owners here at *El Burro* and they let's me bring my dogs."

Regina reached down to grab a floppy pup trying to make off with one of her flip-flops as the Dead Head shed her faded tie-dye shirt for a frolic in the water with the dogs. Her sorry excuse for a swimsuit, one whose elasticity had been stretched to it's limits, made no apologies for exposed private parts. Plunging in with a couple of timid pups, she was soon leading the pack in circles, leaving her new *amigos* to ponder for a while before returning to flop down with her now dripping brood to describe her history as a part of the Grateful Dead Family.

"So why is it that right when I finally become leader of the *Wharf Rats,* Jerry goes and dies?" She must not have expected an answer as she seamlessly went on to extoll her role as caretaker of the special drug free section provided at Grateful Dead shows for recovering addicts. However, now that the band had scattered, she had taken on a new mission in *Baja California.* Reggie and Regina began to recognize an angel as she described her present task of sheltering local strays.

"When the community started bringing me burros and injured animals, my *patron* gave me a couple of acres across from *Playa Coyote* to set up a shelter, so that's my life now."

"Hey, any wharf in a storm" Reggie quipped distractedly. He was again monitoring the bow of the slowly sinking ketch, one portal now slipping closer to the waterline.

"I know where the Captain lives. I'll swing by and remind him to get his bilge pumps working" Angel volunteered, commencing the round-up of her motley pack. "Who knows what contraband may be in peril!"

Loading up the sandy dogs, she made one last solicitation that Regina had a hard time declining. Mr.Sniff and Ms.Chief had been especially attracted to one of her fat bellied pups, a bristly gray one that had curiously reminded Regina of an unlikely cross between a Weenie Dog and a German Shephard. But Reggieq wasn't going for it. Surrendering to destiny, the angel was soon off on her next mission of mercy.

Except for the occasional sound of transport echoing from the highway behind them, after the departure of the station wagon full of dogs, it got really quiet on the beach, even heavenly as they stretched out over sun warmed sand after a swim in the Bahia.

"There sure are a lot of stories along the *Camino Real* ...." Regina mused, distractedly running sand through her fingers like an hourglass.

"*California* dreaming... I know a place we can go...." Reggie breathed into his lover's ear, dribbling suntan oil along the curve of her warm back while he rubbed it around. "How about kayaking over to the Clear Cove...." he suggested seductively.

The shallow water at the cove always revealed delightful glimpses of the natural world that always turned them on. More than just any old scenic point, the stacked rock shelters there along the shore created blissful privacy for outdoor intimacy.
Getting into the mood with Reggie's oily caresses, Regina was easily seduced, while a determined breeze began to fan out across the *Bahia de Conception,* rippling now just a little into one of the portals of the dangerously listing ketch.

Tropic of Cancer

"Wuf!"

"Grrrrrrr...ruf."

It was with an unmistakable stance of triumph that Reggie and Regina hung out over the prow of the party boat *Oceanus*, their *margaritas* flung back at them by the last gasps of the Pacific as they rounded the *Cabo San Lucas*. While the sun hovered over the tip of *California*, playful smooching celebrated the climax of a journey only slightly blemished by aborted past expeditions. They were relishing a moment of victory, fulfilling a quest-initiated years before, finally reaching the citadel of *California* pride, the iconic stone arch looming majestically against the elements and the wild colors of a Pacific sunset.

"Not bad for a couple of old dogs," congratulated Reggie, licking up the last of his drink, now indistinguishable from sea foam dripping down his forehead.

"Time for a refill? Really?" wondered Regina. The cruise advertised limitless *Margaritas*, but there were practical limits.

Helping her tipsy *esposo* back to the upper deck, the band was soulfully recreating Santana's *Oye Como Va* for the gyrating passengers. The Sunset Cruise was breathing life into the party and alternately sucking up anything not attached. Sweaters, *ponchos* and hats were being wildly flung overboard by the wind, while the band played on. The precious hat that their daughter-in-law had entrusted to Reggie's care when she was enlisted into the band, the sombrero that had belonged to her recently departed father, was one of the sacrifices. Reggie cried helplessly as he watched it disappear into the wake, but the *margaritas* continued to flow, the band recruited more volunteers, and the seals cavorted rhythmically as the party cruised by the romantic arches of Lover's Beach, rock and roll sweeping them all the way back into the harbor at *San Lucas*. *El Captaino* and his crew lined up along the plank for well deserved tips as their passengers moved on to their next adventure.

"*Mama mia, mis amigos!* We need to eat." I know a good restaurant *para tacos de pescado. Vamonos*" suggested Red, leading the posse even deeper into the depths of *San Locos* for fish tacos and a serious Mexican hangover.

"Grrrrr, grrrrr" chorused the dogs, going off at the pre-dawn knock on the door of the van. Mr. Sniff and Ms. Chief were always on the lookout.

"Reggie, Regina, psst! *Por favor* - please. Do you have any water? I'm dying!" It was their son Red, pathetically pleading through a back drop of early morning crimson.

"The hotel turned off the water for the night and this *hombre* has a bad headache."

The dogs took the opportunity for a pee and a sniff around the hotel parking lot, while the thirsty Red guzzled down a bottle of *aqua purificada.*

"Good thing you're flying home today" admonished Regina, offering her offspring a dose of Advil. "Doesn't look like you can take too much more fun!"

"Come on up later for a shower, *Tu Stinkos*" offered Red sarcastically, choosing to ignore his mother's cryptic remark. After a week of camping along the dusty *Camino Real* with two dogs, the stinky truth was impossible to ignore.

"Then afterwards let's all walk over for breakfast at The Office before we head to the airport." That suggestion from Red really got the dogs worked up.

"Settle down you *perros*" demanded Reggie, slithering back into his sleeping bag between wagging tails, anxious for a morning romp on the beach. "...at least until dawn."

"I'm stoked that we managed a rendezvous with those guys" reminisced Regina fondly, watching the yellow mini-jet zoom north over the cactus tipped horizon, returning their loved ones to the States.

"*Andale!* Now let's go check out the East Cape. Nic's probably over there by now, enjoying the elements. Plus, these dogs need some space to run!" Wild tail wagging greeted Reggie's welcome suggestion.

Three dusty hours and two military checkpoints later, a 60 km. washboard road finally delivered the Dodge Ram to *Cabo Pulmo*, home of the northern most coral reefs in the Pacific. The road conditions were challenging enough to rebuff an invasion of motor homes and travel trailers. What they found was a collection of the usual suspects; trucks and vans with stateside and Canadian license plates, migrant visitors camping out along the rugged coastline.

"*Guantanamera, guantanamera ...*" sang Reggie, finally delivering his little posse to a sandy bluff, right on the *Tropico de Cancer.* Reaching for the sky behind them, a prickly desert mountain range overlooked the azure coast of the Sea of Cortez, a breathtaking Scenic Point. "Wrap your mind around that!"

"*Ole!*" called out Regina as she released the dogs to charge down the bank of the narrow *arroyo* to meet the locals. They were used to the routine by now.

Being the newcomer requires a good deal of posturing, a complete repertoire of growls, snorting, sniffing and pissing. It was never long though, before they'd all get on to the more important attractions, like old dried-up skeletons of dead fish and shore birds or petrified droppings from other animals.

Meanwhile, Reggie and Regina were doing their own posturing under the curious inspection of an assortment of *gringos,* many of them outfitted with the latest in snorkeling, diving, fishing, kayaking or ultra-lite equipment. An old weathered German couple from Lake Tahoe had an answer to their every question.

"Located right on the Tropic of Cancer, the line-up of reefs here at *Cabo Pulmo* are home to some of the oldest coral heads in North America, possibly 20,000 years old. We're part of a local effort to create a protected zone here, hopefully even a National Park."

Looking around, the newcomers could certainly understand why. The dramatic coastline of stone and sand was nearly pristine. But after searching the bluffs, they were disappointed to discover that Nic wasn't there.

A well-tanned Dread and his tow-headed daughter approached them as they examined Nic's weathered trailer, tucked along the edge of the desert above the rocky cliffs. Four months combing the beaches of *Cabo Pulmo*, while he and his wife from Ontario awaited the birth of their second child, numbered him among Nic Point's intimates. Low tide had emptied the beach and he was heading back to his canopied trailer for a siesta, stopping to explain that Nic had gone over to *Todos Santos* with his craftworks for the next weekend's Art Festival. Although Reggie and Regina were impatient to see their friend, it could wait a few days while they extended their stay on the bluff above Lover's Beach. They had endured exhausting miles on a dusty, potholed, washboard road to get there and now that they had reached Paradise, they were going to make the most of it.

Sucking up the view along with a couple of *Coronas* and an oily little reefer, they made plans to explore the exposed rocks of the now receding tide. Covered with crabs and slippery colonies of sea mosses, giant rock forms were emerging from the clear water like beached seals, dark and wet against white sand. Flocks of seabirds flitted along the edges of the receding tide were hoping for an afternoon snack.

The dogs quickly assembled a posse to join them as they explored the coastline. Following the weather-beaten cliffs toward the point, the posse discovered a geological treasure of colorful rocks and wind sculpted boulders that defied imagination, getting a work-out dodging waves, as they sniffed around piles of weathered driftwood and contemporary debris wedged ominously between the cracks. Wild conventions of leaping Manta Rays churned up the sea along the horizon and the frequent breaching of *California* Gray Whales working their way around the East Cape, were an exciting reminder to the visitors that they were not alone in their migration. The occasional score of a smelly old carcass usually launched another round of peeing and posturing by the dogs until they reached a point where a private beach of sand and rocks worn smooth by the elements, disappeared into a narrow crevice.

Following the dogs through a tight configuration of monumental boulders, they found themselves in a mystical zone. Even the dogs seemed to be enchanted, pausing their sniff to stand by their people respectfully. Subtly emerging from sheer cliff walls, the virtual image of a Buddha figure appeared before them, stoically ready to pour out his infinite wisdom for visitors. Formed by the elements, he described the forces of the natural world, dark veins of mica running from his iconic presence, running through the sand like layers of muscle embracing them in acceptance. Feeling the spirit emanating from the stone face, it was a magical welcome to the Tropic of Cancer.

The first light of mornings brought hungry pelicans, plunging into the clear water to breakfast on boils of fish moving along the coast. Then the golden dawn of sunrise brought fishermen in their colorful pangas to join the fracas, zooming in to net bait fish. Before the wind came up, Reggie and Regina were in the water snorkeling their way between submerged rocks until they reached the edge of deep water. Sunlight created a wonder of prismatic patterns across the reef, revealing a world resplendent with giant corals and fish of all kinds. Rocks crawling with Starfish and schools of Moorish Idols and Sgt. Majors surrounded them curiously as they drifted with the current. Giant Bump-head Parrot fish grazed the reef ravenously above a Leopard shark sleeping in an underwater cave. Brilliant black and yellow Angelfish with incredibly long trailing fins were the most amazing they had ever seen.

One morning the appearance of black fins close behind her loved one had Regina wondering if her life partner was going to become shark chum, until she thankfully realized that it was a pod of dolphins cruising past. By late morning the wind was often up and they would retreat for a mid-day meal before an afternoon walk followed by a siesta. In the evening they would tailgate with other campers making music, usually continuing into the night around a campfire as the cold desert night danced in the shadows cast from the blaze. Luckily, most of the food that had survived the washboard road didn't require refrigeration, since their ice chest soon became useless. If they had realized how remote *Cabo Pulmo* was, they could have been better prepared, but somehow eggs, cans of beans and fish purchased from local fishermen got them through the week.

When the rhythm of the days inevitably brought them to Friday, supplies were running low. Truthfully, they were completely out of everything, groceries, beer, water, even dog food. They had extended their rations as long as they could. Reggie was following a line of low flying Pelicans with binoculars, when he suddenly felt a shift in the tide.

"This has been as close to Paradise as we'll ever get, but I think it's time to get on with this adventure. Remember, the *fiesta* in *Todos Santos* starts *mañana*."

Regina was feeling lazy in the late morning glow of their last warm beers as she contemplated their options.

"Supplies are short..." she agreed, starting to feel hungry... Anyway, I know we'll be back."

No argument from Reggie on that score. They had both fallen in love with the East Cape.

It was barely half an hour of contemplation on a sky of fluffy clouds until they got motivated. Saying farewells to new friends as they rounded up the dog dudes, it was time to follow the sun over the *Sierras* to the Pacific side of the *Tropico de Cancer* and rendezvous with a couple of Scenic Points.

Todos Santos: A Nuclear Wave

    Straddling the Tropic of Cancer, *Todos Santos* is an oasis of epic dimension. Lined by historical brick and adobe buildings crawling with *bougainvillea,* a sense of magic lurks everywhere through the dusty streets surrounding the *Plaza.* Following a troubled history of conquest, epidemics and cultural revolt, the town had become a favorite on the hippy trail, with the cultural mix stirred up to include organic restaurants and coffee shops, galleries, a theatre, a bookstore, and wedged between two Real Estate offices, even a message center offering hourly rates for internet connection.

    The *Plaza* was bursting with activity when Reggie and Regina emerged from their dusty camper van. The Art Festival was in full swing, with the stage packed with young local girls dancing the hula, something they hadn't expected to see in a Mexican village saturated with history.

"So... it's a changing world" they shrugged, crossing the *Plaza* to check out the old parish church.

Senora del Pilar de Todos Santos was perched on the bluff overlooking the *huerta,* where well-tended fields of fruits and vegetables grow between thick stands of palm and the remains of a sugar cane boom from early in the 20th century. Drawn to the historical edifice, Reggie and Regina entered the cool tile foyer to discover a whitewashed alter adorned with fresh flowers on the west end of what appeared to be the original chapel. Leading to a modern structure that had obviously been added more recently, the nave opened into a newer chapel of brilliant light, adorned by angels and curiously echoing with the chords of a familiar contemporary ballad by the Eagles.

"Welcome to the Hotel California, such a lovely place..." A sound check emanating from the culturally infamous Hotel located behind the church, was creating an ironic welcome to *Todos Santos.*

"...What a nice surprise .... Bring your alibis ..." Echoing through open windows on either side of an alter painted with angels, the iconic figures morphed into messengers.

"... You can check out any time you like... but you can never leeeeave ...."

Reggie and Regina weren't sure if the welcome had been a curse or a blessing as they continued their search for Nic Point along the colorful avenues of booths and sound systems strung out below the church, when Mr. Sniff fell in love. Unconvinced by logical explanations, he strained at the leash at every sighting of his new paramour, continually dragging Regina into a tangle of innocent bystanders.

"You're acting like a dog that's headed for a *siesta* in the van" complained Regina, finally distracting her furry friend with a ragged remnant of discarded fish taco, dragging him back to the van anyway.

When they finally found Nic, he was tanned and grinning from behind a wild display of his artwork. Combining natural elements, wired and cemented together with colorfully painted found objects, his crazy configurations were spread out on a bright Mexican blanket surrounded by a curious crowd.

"Nooooort!" The familial greeting immediately got their friend's attention.

"*Mis amigos!* We meet again." Even though his friends from the Faire were crisp around the edges, they could still rely on an enthusiastic welcome from C.Nic Point.

"*Que honda* - what's up, Nic? Your work looks great."

"Hey! You're right on time for the Nuclear Wave!"

Nic went on to explain what seemed like an episode out of The X-Files. Evidentially, the last time the French had conducted a nuclear test on a remote atoll in the South Pacific, the seismic wave extending across the ocean had created a monster swell along the coast of *Baja California*.

" Dudes, there was another test a few days ago and now we're preparing for another nuclear wave. The posse is camping out at Cerritos beach, and we'll be ready for it when it gets here."

"Are you *loco de la cabeza?*" Nic's old hippy friends could barely even imagine this kind of excitement about a nuclear explosion.

Every rise in *Baja California* offers another spectacular scenic point and as the dusty Dodge Ram left the paved road at the top of a hill a little south of *Todos Santos* the morning after the festival, Reggie and Regina paused to glory at the panoramic sweep of beach and surf. With sets lined up to the horizon like ripples on the edge of a dime, *Punta Cerritos,* was a beacon for West Coast surfers.

After driving cautiously down the dusty washboard road leading to the famous Pacific point, the newcomers watched incredulously as a speeding panga jettisoned toward the beach, pulling up the motor to escape seeming disaster at only the very last second. Ploughing well up onto the sand, they ready to unload plastic containers of fish on ice, for sale to waiting merchants.

"Let's see if they will sell us some fish" Reggie suggested, jumping out of the van and charging toward the fishermen along with a cadre of other beach scavengers.

Pelicans, gulls and red headed vultures were living large as the beach filled up with discarded fish heads and guts. While Reggie bargained for fish, a hefty pickup pulled out onto the beach to drag the *panga* to safety. A familiar figure jumped out of the cab. No surprise, it was C.Nic Point.

"Hey *amigos*! Are you ready for the Big One?" With a sense of destiny, they embraced the hospitality.

"Park on up by that One Ton O 'Mayhem" he directed, pointing to a beat-up van stacked with surf equipment, blending into the edge of the desert just beyond an improvised Surf Shop. "That's my *amigo's* rig and he and the family will make room for you to set up camp. Can't wait for you to meet Little Rip."

Los Perros were happy to finally have some space to run after a night cooped up in the van, leaping out onto the sand to commence the usual formalities along with a pack of noisy beach dogs. Reggie began the process of setting up camp and the smell of fresh brew was soon blending with the sweet scent of fresh rolled while they settled down to check out the scene.

Rumors about the nuclear event had created quite a gathering. The surf camp had temporarily moved to higher ground in anticipation of the monster waves, putting a serious premium on camping space. Mingling their pieced together encampments with the more seasonal nomads in older model RV's and trailers with the usual mix of Stateside and Canadian plates, the makeshift arrangement had created the sense of a carnival. Vendors wandered along the beach with home cooked tamales, blankets and trinkets. The surfers waxed their boards in preparation, ready to head out to the point at the first sign of a swell. The posse of tawny bodies squinting out from beneath tousled dreads had one eye on the horizon at all times. The view from the edge of the desert was awesome with a spectacle of stratified clouds radiating out from the horizon.

"Hey, look out there!" Regina excitedly pointed to several whale spouts just off the break where they seemed to be mingling, flukes twisting above the waves for a glimpse of the festivities.

"Oh yeah, they check by every day" explained a voice from somewhere deep inside the One Ton O' Mayhem. Then the voice abruptly rolled out onto the sand, emphatically wrestling a *Modelo* beer can from a red headed three-year old.

"Gnarly grip you little grommet! Give it up!" But before Mother Mayhem could get it, the beer was in the sand and the little dude was on to his next conquest; feeding pineapple pie to the dogs.

The women that accompanied these winter safaris were as buff as the dudes, seemingly able to thrive on a diet of fish and beer and *boleos* delivered from town daily by enterprising local entrepreneurs. Mrs. Mayhem was looking good in a skimpy bikini top with a colorful sarong slung casually around her slender hips as she opened a can of JUMEX for Little Rip.

Still Dreaming California

Ms.Chief and Mr. Sniff had created their own usual mayhem upon arrival, but Little Rip easily exploded their ritual, scattering the whole pack of dogs with a mighty "Oi chi-jua-jua!" Luckily, Regina managed to divert most of the pack, encouraging them to follow her and Little Rip out to the edge of the sand to entertain the whales with crazy antics.

Just as Reggie finished up his first brew, the gutsy lyrics of SUBLIME pulled up through a cloud of dust and the Boss Mayhem himself leaped out of a very beat-up TOYOTA pick-up. A dude, with his trucker hat on backwards and his bleached-out baby dreads hanging over his shades, he was clearly at a pinnacle. Having grown up in the SoCal surf scene, he was only remotely like any dude from "*Bay Watch*". Surviving the test of the elements in the rugged landscape of *Baja*, he had graduated from that long ago, now making a transition to year-round living in *Baja California*.

"We didn't wanna run out of beer" spit out the Bro in a thick SoCal drawl, as he began unloading enough supplies to last through the big event. The tailgate party was on when Mrs. Mayhem freaked. A small goat skinned and peering out of a plastic bucket emerged from the back of the pickup along with the cases of *Ballenas*.

"*El Chuppacabra* or not, I'm fuckin 'roasting this goat for dinner tonight" declared the Boss Mayhem, stubbornly refusing to get superstitious over an old Mexican Super-Thug myth of a giant human like vampire sneaking around sucking the blood out of young goats. Never mind that this kid was laying limp in a bucket with two giant punctures in his neck.

"Well, I'm not going to eat any of it" scoffed Mrs. Mayhem. "That was Little Rip's pet goat. Anyway, how could we eat anything that may have been sucked by a vampire? Yuk!"

"We would have had to drain the blood anyway even if we had planned to eat it. Except for the blood, it's untouched. Let's not be wasteful."

Determinedly heading off to gather wood for the barbecue, this last assertion was punctuated by a yelp as the Boss stomped on a spiny cactus chunk camouflaged by beach debris. With the Boss dude out of commission for a while, Nic and Reggie got to work on the campfire. Countdown preparations for the big wave were happening up and down the beach encampment while over at the trailer park the RV crowd was obliviously retiring for their evening martinis.

"I wonder if that will be us in a few years, raising the martini flag over our condos every afternoon after a game of golf?"

"I don't think so!" chorused the posse, cracking open a few beers while they commenced a group howl.

The rise of a spectacular full moon over the desert skyline behind Cerritos beach was prismatic around the edges, as Neptune, Saturn and Uranus joined in harmonic convergence along the Tropic of Cancer into a purple sky.

The posse partied on after the barbecue of Little Rip's goat. The guitars came out and the entourage of dogs got settled into their spots around the campfire, contentedly chewing on various dis-guarded body parts. Rotating shifts stayed on the lookout for early signs of the swell, as a heavy session of reasoning unfolded.

"Paving *El Camino Real* might have been an impossible dream for Portola and the Padres in 1768" Nic mused, "but that is exactly what has brought so much change to *California* in the last 25 years. I admit I love to come here, but too many visitors are really impacting the environment of this place."

Quoting some astronomical prices for desert property with no water rights, he continued his speculation, directing his gaze toward the blackening desert silhouette.

"It takes hundreds of years for a big *Cordon* cactus to develop" the Boss sighed, "and only a few pesos for a dozer to clear a *hectare* in an afternoon."

"At the rate they are sub-dividing, especially at *Cabo*, there may be a day when you won't even be able to see the ocean anymore." With towering hotels planned all along the corridor between *San Jose* and *San Lucas*, Nic Point was of course worried about the views.

"Anyway, where are they going to get enough water for all those golf courses?"

The implications hovering over a question like that brought some sober contemplation around the fire while Reggie strummed a few melancholy chords on his guitar. Orion towered above them as Venus slipped into the Pacific when the circle grew to include Dr. Woozle, just arrived from *Agua Verde* where he spent most of his winters. A musician with a photographic memory, he knew all the words to every song. Immediately diving into Bob Dylan's *Like a Rolling Stone* without forgetting even one verse before teaming up with Reggie for an intense rendition of Barry McGuire's *Eve of Destruction,* followed by a series of Beach Boys all-time favorites, the spirit was festive.

"What about the invasion of RVs? We just explored the highway all the way down *California.* The *Vagabundos* are all over the *Baja* beaches. If you can drive there, they do and then park their rigs as close as they can to the shoreline, maybe so that no one else can enjoy it." Regina was getting worked up as Reggie interrupted her story.

"Then up goes the satellite dish so they can stay inside and watch FOX-News!" That got the posse howling again and got the dogs worked up for a sniff out on the moonlit desert-scape where they headed off a herd of wild burros attempting to graze through the camp.

"A few years ago you could dig a bucket of clams in ten minutes. Now you mostly find them when the vendors bring them to you" Dr. Woozle lamented before breaking into another song.

"Fuck me Dude, it's because of the government!" Stories from Boss Mayhem were usually well spiced. "Japan did a deal with the Mexican government for a new telecommunication system in exchange for shellfish rights. They fuckin 'scraped the seafloor 'til there was nothing left but piles of seashells on the desert! *Pinche pendejos!* It will take years to recover."

"I haven't seen many turtles either. Is that seasonal?" questioned Regina, tossing another hefty piece of driftwood onto the fire to send sparks circling to the stars.

"Oh yeah, they come to lay their eggs on the dunes at the end of the year, but there are only a few that come now" answered Mrs. Mayhem. "Those abandoned buildings over by the fish camp at *Punta Lobos* were the processing plant. The turtles are supposed to be protected, but the locals still collect the eggs as a delicacy and so many people camp and drive on the beaches that the hatchlings have a hard time making it to the water. They get stranded in the tire grooves and become an easy meal for the birds. Little Rip and I carried a lot of them to safety after they hatched last season."

Little Rip was oblivious to the prestige this last revelation awarded him as his *Madre* carried him off to the One Ton O'Mayhem and the sleep he would need before the next day's big adventure. But the posse didn't miss a beat as Reggie and the Doctor played on until the moon was high in the sky.

Still Dreaming California

The rhythm of the waves changed with the dawn. Years of hanging out along the Pacific coast waters of *California* had developed a keen sense of synergy among the hard-core surfers, and simultaneously they felt the big event approaching. Nic was stoking a corner of last nights fire, brewing coffee for the sleepier campers, mixing in a hit of tequila, "for the nerves", when the high energy peaked with the rising sun.

Checking out the beach scene, Nic noticed that many legendary surfers had filtered in with the sunrise and along with them, lots of wanna-be surfers there for the chance of hanging with legendary professionals. He was glad that he had brought along some extra rolls of film. If ever there was a photo-op, this was clearly one of them and he was hoping for a winning shot of the "Big One".

Grabbing his gear, he made his way up the rocky cliff for a better vantage point. Setting up his tripod on the very edge of the cliff overlooking the vast Pacific panorama, it was an optimal location from which to study the horizon. Incoming wave sets fanned out to form huge crescents across the Pacific, now dotted with a multitude of surfers whooping it up on the radical wave sets that were developing, thrilling Nic with anticipation, ready for a documentary shot of epic proportion.

"Maybe something for SURFER magazine…" Hoping to get lucky.

They were ready for the Nuclear Wave. It was warming up on the beach, getting irie with a mix of Ranchero and Reggae music filtering out over the surfer scene. Inspired to hone their skills, children were sliding along the shoreline over the wet sand on skim boards, more often than not plunging head over heel into the wash. Nic had to smile as he focused in on a shot of Little Rip practicing with his boogie board close to shore as his Dad headed out with his own freshly waxed board.

Turning back to the horizon he saw a change, noticing the swells spreading out wide and glassy, taking longer to gather themselves. He wasn't the only one to notice. The experienced Dudes headed their line-up further out while the novices lined-up closer to shore, intimidated by the impending swell.

Nic got situated behind his zoom lens to survey the line-up. There was Van Johnson, and it looked like the Bros. over from Hawaii. And was that Fat Bastard from Santa Cruz?

"Hey, wazzup....." he muttered to himself. His attention had been diverted by an alarming scenario.

Little Rip was making his way out over the rocky point with his boogie board. Waving to his Dad whose attention was on the horizon, he took the biggest leap of his short life and began paddling out to where the set of nuclear waves was gathering momentum.

C.Nic Point dropped down the cliff like Spiderman. Seizing a board from a hesitant young surfer, he ran down to the point and leaped into the water with mighty intention, a mountain of water rising around him. Could he make it in time? But a few paddle lengths away, Little Rip was already making a new friend.

"Hi there Little Dude. Allow me to introduce myself. I'm Mike Doyle, Surf Legend. I designed that board you're using and it looks like we're going to give it a big test. Here comes the Nuclear Wave and we're gonna take it together." There was no other option at this point. Grabbing Rip's tow line, he turned to catch the wave.

"HOLD ON LITTLE RIP! HERE WE GOoooooo........!"

The rest of the lineup gave way as Nic slipped into a backup position. Calls of encouragement greeted them as they caught the

Still Dreaming California

epic wave as a team, dropping down the steep slope just as the giant wave began to crest, falling into a giant tube.

"WE'RE GOING TUBULAR!" Mike shouted as they crouched to slip in, shredding through the curl with Little Rip between them and it was high five all the way into surf history. The Nuclear Wave had surpassed all expectations. Wading out for her son through the frothy boil as the giant wave swept them up the beach, Mrs. Mayhem was jubilant. Fate or whatever, at three years old Little Rip had already become a legend.

The carnival atmosphere had moved on and the footprints left from the nuclear event were being erased by the elements as Reggie and Regina hunkered down in their hoodies to watch the fading day. Scattered puffy clouds turned florescent pink before organizing themselves into a pasture of prismatic zebra stripes blending into the golden *California* horizon. A herd of horses cantered along the surf line, evidently happy to almost have the beach back to themselves.

The sky was shifting to purple as a field of diamonds began twinkling quantum messages in harmony with the Reggae rhythms of Bob Marley wafting out from the Surf Shop up the beach. Reggie was strumming along.

"*He who feels it, knows it....*" and they were feeling it.

The Tropic of Cancer had created a new paradigm.

Extending like roots all the way through their toes as they dug their feet into the still warm sand; hearing it as they answered the call of an osprey heading home on the evening wind; ready for it as they settled in for the brewing moonrise. Recognizing the metaphors, they realized that they had been scooped up by destiny. Reggie and Regina intrinsically understood that their path would always lead them back to the *Tropico de Cancer*

Santiago

"We can add this to the list" Reggie meekly complained to his *amigos* as they helplessly gazed out over the flooded *arroyo*.

"Stick ya, prick ya, poke ya... and now stranded on the wrong side of an *arroyo*!" There was no way around it or over it. Humbled by the natural world, the *gringos* were still fine tuning their Mexican experience.

Dan and Yolanda had agreed in the beginning that it was "all about location, location, location" when Reggie and Regina had found the battered adobe brick house for sale in *Baja California Sur*. Forming a partnership with these long time Renaissance Faire comrades who also shared their love for *California*, *La Casa* had been one of the last best deals on the East Cape. Perched on the bluff with eight palm trees on the property overlooking the Sea of Cortez, the *amigos* hadn't allowed its neglected condition to diminish their enthusiasm. They had already torn down the battered patio *pergola*, replaced doors and installed screens. The rusted water heater leaning against the outside wall of the bathroom miraculously continued to supply hot water. Plans were underway for a new *bodega* - garage. Now they were yearning for some big-time color befitting a house in Mexico.

The newcomers had noticed the ominous skyline of blackened cumulus when they began their late afternoon mission to COMEX for paint supplies, but it hadn't registered at the time since it wasn't raining yet where they were and they had not yet experienced the signs of an impending flash flood.

"From now on, if it looks like it's raining in the mountains... it probably is" Dan pointlessly lectured.

Evidently triggered by a torrential mountain thunderstorm, the road across the *arroyo* leading to *La Casa* had now been swallowed up by a flash flood of raging muddy water. A BIMBO delivery van was perched precariously near the waterline on a small rise midway across the *arroyo*, watched by a growing crowd of stranded motorists on both sides, who seemed to all know one another. The mood was almost festive as they mingled patiently on the embankment above the flood, *cervezas* magically appearing to fortify the spirit as the rain intensified. The general consensus seemed to be that the flood would not recede before midnight. Soaking wet and getting hungry, Yolanda suggested they seek shelter in nearby Santiago to wait out the flood.

One of the old mission towns, that dreary evening *Santiago* was shrouded in dusk. Slowly circling the deserted plaza surrounded by old colonial buildings, the *amigos* finally noticed a dim light emerging from one obscure doorway. A short sprint through the rain and their prayers were answered. A single dim lightbulb hanging from the shop ceiling was a ray of hope for the bedraggled refugees.

Sparsely arranged in random order, the small *tienda* appeared to have one of everything. Tripping over a battered toy fire truck hidden in shadow, Regina found herself staring into the hapless face of a big blue Teddy Bear. Oversized and overlooked for too many seasons, he was leaning dejectedly between an aluminum tamale pot and a Hello Kitty cosmetic bag.

"Hey! We need some new cutlery" Dan exclaimed, brazenly running his finger along a massive machete blade. Luckily it wasn't very sharp.

"*Hola! Hola!*" Feeling vulnerable, it seemed oddly disrespectful shouting their presence to such an historical edifice.

"***Que paso!***" they called a little louder, while the Virgin of Guadalupe stared down at them with compassion from a framed picture above a darkened doorway.

When an elderly *Señora* emerged wiping her hands on her apron, she made no apologies for her tardiness. Directing them to a clothes rack squeezed in behind a display of Sponge Bob *pinatas*, they happily found three jackets among her meager inventory. One of them would have to be satisfied with a *poncho*.

The exiles looked very patriotic as they paraded into *Resaurante El Palomar* wearing new jackets in the colors of the Mexican flag; slender Yolanda in a child's turquoise sweater; Reggie in a women's white fleece jacket; Regina in a bright red, size extra-large hoodie with an embroidered white emblem of a bear titled "OSO" and numbered "2".

"Hey Poncho! This is our spot." That is when Dan had become Poncho with his new blanket sweater. He and Reggie had long been joking about opening an entertainment venue and calling it *Poncho and Lefty's*. Implicitly, that meant that Reggie had to be Lefty but since he was right-handed, he wasn't ready to commit. The trophy Buck hanging over the fireplace was indifferent as their host pulled a table and chairs close enough to the hearth for his soggy guests to feel the heat. They all ordered *margaritas*.

"Making the decision to wait out the storm in *Santiago* was the right thing to do" Regina confessed to Yolanda, wondering why she had been so hesitant when her friend had made the suggestion. "Watching the flood wouldn't have made it go down any faster anyway."

Aiming her still damp feet closer to the blazing fireplace while she studied the trophy animals adorning the walls, she began fantasizing what it would be like to meet a monster boar out on the desert. Providing shelter from the storm, faded framed photos made it apparent that the old *cantina* had a long history of hospitality. Pictures of Bing Crosby and Bob Hope with Dwight Eisenhower and a lot of other conspicuous posers were reminders of an era when Hollywood stars had enjoyed hunting expeditions to *Baja California* and the sleepy mission town of *Santiago* had been a destination point for the rich and famous.

Reggie and Poncho were dramatically describing the scene down in the *arroyo*, stranded with the masses by the flash flood that had altered all their plans, when the story, the fire and the *tequila* began to create a cozy circle with companions of chance. They met the woman who now lived in Bing Crosby's old house just down the street. They learned that the indigenous *Pericue* population had known *Santiago* as *Ainini*. Jesuit *Padre* Lorenzo Carranco had been martyred in the Indian Rebellion of 1734.

"Hey Bro', I think I'm your *homey*" exclaimed a middle aged man that had settled in with them by the fire to talk story.

"I'm originally from *Alta California,* but I've been living here for sixteen years with my Mexican wife" he explained. I rent my house there in Rio Del Mar and it supports me and my family here. I make it back every so often to take care of business, but less and less frequently. It's *muy loco* what's happening to that area, crazy with traffic, crazy with congestion, and crazy prices! But hey Bro, good memories" he shrugged, distractedly twisting his mustache. "Did you ever hang at the *Chateau Liberte*?"

While Reggie and their new *compa* started down a list of possible mutual acquaintances, even the legendary Jack Cassidy who had frequented that area of the Santa Cruz Mts., Regina's attention became focused on the familiar way he told his story.

"Yes" she thought, this was indeed their *homey*. It would've been hard to guess at first, considering their first impression of him as a local *campasino* with his Pancho Villa mustache and muddy work clothes, stopping by for *cerveza* on his way home from the fields, which it turned out he actually was.

"My wife's family goes back to the Sacred Expedition. In return for service, their family was granted a massive tract of land far up in the *Sierras* above *Bahia Magdalena*. Many of her ancestors never even left the *Rancho* in their entire lives!"

He became very animated as he continued to describe the remote *Rancho* that had been self-sustaining over generations. He was obviously proud to have married into such a historically connected family whose blood now flowed through the veins of his own children.

"Her family uses a sun sign traced back to their Spanish heritage," he further informed the new arrivals, describing that symbol created by some remote ancestor incorporated into a magnificent tile floor at the old hacienda.

"You should see them dance across that floor. They play and sing like the *Gypsy Kings*!" With that he broke into song and the bar tender brought another round along with more fuel for the fire. The road might have been open by then, but the journey back to *La Casa* would have to first acquiesce to Mexican hospitality.

"How does your family like the States?" Regina quizzed innocently when their new acquaintance had finally paused to drink. The question got an unexpected reaction.

"Crossing the border is humiliating for them, especially now with all the Homeland Security crap! I hate putting them through that experience. It just makes everyone feel bad for no reason. My kids are not drug smugglers or terrorists!" he declared emphatically, pausing for effect.

"So, I'm Mexican now." The way he jumped to his feet let the *Amigos* think that the conversation was over.

Yolanda twirled her still damp curls while Poncho pulled his blanket a little closer in the silence that followed their *compa's* self-righteous outburst. They didn't agree with border profiling, but as Americans, they understood their own complicity. Uncomfortable, Regina was certain that the trophy Buck mounted on the wall next to the fireplace had changed its mounted stance to stare down at them.

It was yet another story from an ex-pat affected by U.S.A. fear mongering. Mexican and Central Americans were frustrated by the racist policy since 9-11 and stereotyping within a punitive migration system that was threatening stability on both sides of the border. The *Amigos* were changing their perspective as they met ex-patriots fleeing American economic insecurity and Capitalism on steroids. Not just Snowbirds escaping cold winters for a few weeks, now that they had their own place in *Baja California,* they were meeting the growing ex-patriate community south of the border.

"But hey, nothing personal *amigos*" their new friend mercifully declared. "My daughter's *Quincienara* is next month and I'd like to invite you. It will be her fifteenth birthday and it's traditional to have a big celebration. My wife's whole family will be coming down from the mountains and for some of them, it'll be their first trip away from the *Rancho*. The fiesta will be ragin ' with *comidas Mexicano y musica* all weekend!"

"Mexican food and music!"

It was simply an invitation to a party, but to the *gringos*, it felt like a chance for redemption.

Espectaculares!

The horizon was wildly changing color while four *amigos* sprawled on the shoreline watching the sunset gather in a spectacular swirling sky. Horses standing in the lagoon seemed unimpressed as they continued grazing, while legions of wild avians headed home in formation.

Reggie and Regina were entertaining visitors from Oregon and it had been another glorious day of beach combing. That was the only activity that Jean and Skeeter had wanted for their vacation on the Sea of Cortez and relishing the solitude, she and Skeeter had been content spending every day exploring along the glorious East Cape shoreline of sandy dunes, lagoons and estuaries, watching the natural world and collecting treasure.

"I want them all" Skeeter whined at Jean's insinuation, that there were choices to be made.

"You can pick up all the shells on the beach but you can't have them all. Practice making choices and be satisfied with those choices" she insisted

Jean was being a pragmatist because there actually were practical considerations. After two weeks of exploring the *Bahia*, Skeet had gathered enough treasure to fill multiple suitcases. Shells, driftwood, bones and sea glass, it was a trove that he wanted to take back home for making mobiles to sell at the Saturday Market.

Jean was collecting too, but her treasures were metaphors. She was painting the vistas that caught her attention as they explored the *Bahia*. Using rich pastel colors, the pages of her tablet held her seaside memories of broad beaches laying beneath horizons of spiraling cloudscapes.

"What do you think of that!"

Skeeter's tone rapidly brought Regina to an upright position, but scanning the horizon was a disappointment. Her timing had been off all afternoon. While her *compadres* had scored multiple sightings of whales breaching and spouting, she'd inevitably been distracted by other things.

"Not a whale this time!" her *amigos* chorused, directing her focus up the beach instead. Not just the sight of horses gleefully running along the shoreline, the vision included four young children frolicking along behind them. The spectacle was captivating.

"It looks like a circus" Regina mused with good reasoning. The children were flipping and rolling, summersaulting and cartwheeling through the sand towards them as if they were scheduled for their own exclusive performance. The dogs tilted their heads curiously, not sure whether to bark or join in the fun as Elvis, Jose Manuel, Angel Gabrielle and America Melina arrived like a mirage into their midst.

"Ole', ole'!"

Applause is universal and the children responded to the *gringos* with wide smiles. The boys immediately challenged each other to feats of daring with two double and then triple and finally five consecutive backwards and forwards summersaults, while little America Melina filled in with cartwheels, her gauzy yellow dress catching the wind like a beautiful parasail.

When they were ready to catch their breath, the children mistook the simple Spanish words that the *gringos* used to gain a few facts, for fluency, proceeding to bombard them with information and questions of their own.

"Sounds like we could catch the show in the neighboring village tonight" they finally agreed before the children started to lose interest. But then, with a resume of early childhood education, Skeet blasted through the language barrier by starting a massive sandcastle. The dogs and children gleefully joined in. Sand was flying everywhere under the sunset until the gathering twilight reminded them all that it was time to get ready for the show.

" Madre de Dios!" Reggie blurted out in amazement.

The shabby appearance of the Big Tent was a dose of reality for the *gringos*. In a flash they realized that Stateside expectations were unrealistic for the itinerant troops of performers drifting through the countryside entertaining the small villages of rural Mexico. Far from disappointed though, they weren't about to retreat. Like an ocular hallucination, the spectacle was magnetic. The visual dichotomy of a sudden arrival of longhorns parading in single file toward them was enough to dispel any hesitancy.

"This synchronism is irrefutable" Skeet proclaimed, leading the way to a dusty van with *"ESPECULARES" painted* on it's side.

Familiar voices soon greeted them from the late model van parked out front of the tattered tent. Enthusiastically tumbling out of every window, the children from that afternoon's beach performance welcomed them, happily posing in front of the big bright *"ESPECTACULARES"*, while Skeeter shot photos from every angle. Angel Gabrielle continued to pose proudly until his very pregnant *Madre* finally insisted that he get ready for the performance.

Pulling aside the tattered entrance into the dilapidated tent they surveyed twenty or so assorted chairs surrounding the ring in a single row. America Melina's painted face beckoned them shyly from a torn gap behind a grouping of white plastic lawn chairs at the far end of the row. No popcorn or cotton candy, the *gringos* took their seats and made themselves comfortable while other locals filed in with their families.

Dressed humbly in worn street clothes, the ringmaster warmed up the audience, promising spectacular feats of daring over a fuzzy sound system. Wandering toddlers paraded boldly into the sandy plastic ring while big sisters and brothers obediently retrieved them. Remnants of a missing ceiling hung forlornly, making a window for the full moon and also allowing balls from the game across the street to intermittently sail into their midst. The show was about to begin as the dust settled and the lights were adjusted to reveal the painted faces of the performers peering from around sagging curtains. The sound system crackled as they turned up the volume.

Elvis burst across the floor first, with a quadruple set of summersaults and a double twist at the end! He was soon joined by Jose Manuel, costumed as the clown that would keep them laughing through the whole show with crazy antics, while his sister and brothers truly astounded the audience with acrobatics, juggling and crazy tricks on unicycles that looked like they were going to come unglued at any moment.

"I thought that I was the King of Duct Tape" Skeet whispered confidentially, "but these guys are way over the top!" It was obvious that the *familia* was looking forward to better times financially, with their props and costumes in poor repair. But in no way did that distract from their talented performances.

"Elvis is probably the best juggler I have ever seen anywhere!" Jean exclaimed as his tight set came to a climactic close in a barrage of spinning fire.

"Don't you wish that they could perform at the Faire?" Regina fantasized, exploding in wild applause. "The Shire would just eat them up!"

"What would that be like?" Reggie appraised the possibility, trying to imagine the children in 15th Century Renaissance regalia, bridging more than just a cultural barrier.

"Choices have already been made for these children" Jean reminded them as they got to their feet.

"Hey! It could happen. I could arrange a gig at the Country Fair too!" Skeet was emphatic about the possibilities. "You know this talented family has a great future. Let them be dreamers!"

But Skeet soon realized that he was letting himself be delusional again.

Dropping generous tips on their way out of the tent, joyful waves from the *"FAMILIA ESPECTACULARES"* made it obvious that they were already living their dream.

Dancing on the Edge

Regina met Anni at the weekly Farmers Market.

Dripping with creativity, the Saturday event is a magnet for locals and visitors wanting a colorful glimpse into the diverse community spirit of San Jose del Cabo, BCS, Mexico. Spread out on a circular carpet of lawn on the edge of the lagoons below the Art District of old San Jose, Reggie and Regina were stoked to discover the local counterculture event.

Taking a wide glance around the market, locally grown fresh produce and regional foods along with art and music, made a colorful kaleidoscope of activity. Vendors were grouped in shaded areas around a perimeter of booths, while a sound system throbbed Latin rhythms from under a big tree at the heart of the action. Surrounded by young people performing with hula hoops and acrobatics, people young at heart were dancing too.

"*Bueno!* A Mexican hippy scene!" The visitors from the East Cape were thankful to their new *amigos,* locals who were introducing them to the popular event. "We're happy to see that the creative spirit is alive and flourishing in *Cabo.*"

A couple with deep Mexican roots, Carlos and Wendy had spent decades in the States. Once the owners of an exotic aquarium store in L.A., burned to the ground during the Rodney King riots, they welcomed a dose of the stateside culture that they were so familiar with, while generously sharing slices of the Mexico that they loved and knew so well. Teaching their new *gringo* friends the more subtle nuances of Mexican culture was sometimes embarrassing for Reggie and Regina, but with grace and humor, Carlos and Wendy managed to turn even their most ignorant blunders into insightful lessons.

"Careful what you pay," Carlos joked with his usual playful humor. *"De chivo los tamales:* Beware of goat tamales! Things here at the market might not always be what they are claimed ..." he advised, as his new friends got ready to explore the market and it's treasure of creativity.

A vivacious artist with an interesting accent, Anni was waxing poetic before an enchanted audience of admirers seduced by her brilliant display of silver jewelry. Regina squeezed in to catch some of her story. Arranged in an iconic setting of elements from the natural world, her jewelry reflected the spirit of her vision.

"I find inspiration from the magic present in everyday Life; through the joy and pain of being a human on this earth in these times; through nature, the arts, friends and family."

Regina especially had her eye on a set of lotus blossom earrings, but Reggie was signaling from a table where the posse was feasting on freshly prepared *empanadas*. A Reggae rhythm began weaving its own enchantment from the heart of the Market as Regina realized that the rest of Anni's story would have to wait.

"Do it Reggie! It will make you a better man." Regina joined them just as Carlos was convincing Reggie to follow up on an offer from the band. PURA VIDA would be playing again that night at HAVANAS, a local nightclub, and after a conversation about their mutual love for Reggae music, had invited Reggie to sit in for a couple of songs.

"HAVANAS is along the Corridor, not far from our *casa*. You can stay with us overnight. Then we can take you to the *Municipal Mercado* for breakfast tomorrow morning." Wendy was always generous and encouraging, especially when it came to the arts. A *Baja California* native, she had worked in the film industry in L.A. before life in the States had become so insane that they had decided to return to their roots in Mexico.

"We'll be your groupies!" Wendy's hopeful giggle was very convincing.

How could Reggie resist? And now that Regina was talking about a jeweler with lotus earrings, staying another day would be an opportunity for them all to nurture new friendships while learning more about *San Jose del Cabo,* an original mission town, a charming colonial city saturated with history.

※

Showing her original jewelry at local hotels, markets and Festivals, Regina was learning that Anni was also a teacher on a mission to bring healing to the Earth through meditation, music and dance. Squeezing in a visit from Regina between teaching a morning Chi Kung class at the local Community Center and an afternoon at the *Fiesta Americana* where she regularly displayed her jewelry on a rustic cart, Regina was there to purchase the lotus earrings that she had seen at the market.

Watching Anni manage her busy life with cheerful enthusiasm amidst her charming living space, offered many clues to how she maintained her creative spirit; the patio was overflowing with tropical plants, an outdoor freeform shower area dripped with ambiance, reflections danced from the many crystals hanging from every window. Spiritual icons throughout her garden set a mood of peaceful contemplation. The family dog was an adorable tangle of curls and so was Anni.

Annette Laurel Scott was born in East London, South Africa into a musical family where she and her siblings shared their early life experiences surrounded by creativity. Drama, music and dance were early influences that later led her to university studies in Music Therapy in Cape Town. During a travel sabbatical, backpacking around Europe, she began making bead earrings to finance her travels and learning on the road from different crafts persons, she successfully perfected her craft. She met her daughter's father while traveling along the rivers of northern Brazil, continuing to Peru, Ecuador and Colombia.

"He was a jeweler from Chile. He taught me how to solder with silver, which took my jewelry to another level. Also, the music of South America became a big attraction for me. On my return to South Africa, I continued my studies and that's when I discovered my love for improvisation."

This realization led Anni to develop *"Creative Music and Movements"* classes and inspired her to further develop her skills as a Musical Storyteller.

"So Anni, how did you find your way to this community?"

"Our daughter was born in Ecuador. Then we were a year back to Africa before coming here. During that time I started to attend retreats with Carlos de Leon in Mexico City, studying the spiritual traditions of Buddhism, Tantric Hindu, Cabala and Taoism and he became my spiritual teacher. We spent most of our time between Mexico City, *Michoacan* and *Cabo*. Then a few years ago I became a Mexican citizen and made my base here in *Cabo* where there are great opportunities as a jeweler, as well as for all the courses, retreats and private consultations that I offer."

"How do you find time for so much inspiration?" Regina was amazed by the way Anni was balancing a shower, hanging up a load of laundry, finishing details on several necklaces and packing *comidas* for a snack later, while still managing to communicate with her visitor sincerely and from the heart.

"Everything flows from daily practice and intention. I am presently focusing on Chi Kung, an ancient Chinese energy practice, body-mind integrative therapy, and the Sacred Circle Dance. I provide a space where people can come together in meditation, song and dance, experience joy, presence and communion for the healing of ourselves, our communities and our Earth." Pausing to caress the dog, Anni signaled that she needed to get going, handing over the Lotus earrings with an invitation.

"Would you like to join my next Circle Dance Retreat?"

It was an election year in the States. Up until then, snowbirds and ex-pats of all political persuasions had agreed to leave politics at the border in favor of focusing on the experiences that they all shared as visitors in a foreign land, fascinated with a new culture. But recent political discussions had become toxic. A recent memorial for a much loved local gringo had exploded into a confrontation over American energy policies. True red and true blue, the conversation quickly escalated past science, into ideological warfare, hemorrhaging any semblance of rationality. Soon after Reggie had been served with a vicious "Friendship Divorce", delivered online with enough verbal diarrhea to possibly even choke a FOX News political commentator!

Regina was wondering if she would be able to suspend her frustration in time to heal the Earth? Winding into the towering *Sierras* on a precarious, gravel road, she was on her way to Anni Scott's *Circle Dance Retreat*. Challenged emotionally, she suspected that she might have become hostage to a simmering personal paradox. Bringing unwanted feelings of anger and confusion with her, where was the love?

But that inner turmoil would have to wait. Regina was becoming anxious as she navigated the narrowing path between steep canyon walls and a precipitous drop into a boulder strewn wrecking yard. At one point, she was traversing an eroded creek bed over roughhewn wooden planks. Barely passable, even with 4-wheel-drive, the road suddenly careened through a pile of mountain ruble, casting her into deep shadow. Regina shuddered to imagine the avalanche that had created it.

Thrust by the pressure of plate tectonics, the majestic *Sierra de las Lagunas* Mountains displayed the power of colliding continents. Representing millions of years, layers of the continental shelf were tipped on their side, a testament to the eternal. Towering granite peaks up to 7100 feet high form the jagged skyline of the Mexican peninsula state of *Baja California Sur.* Even while welcoming the opportunity of exploring one of its dramatic mountain canyons, Regina understood why the area had remained so isolated. Close to inaccessible as she crept deeper into the heart of the canyon, *Weeping Juniper* trees tenaciously clung to sheer rock walls and yellow *Palo de Arco* was blooming everywhere. There were no visible power lines, instead she noticed solar installations perched on the roofs of the old Ranchos and evidentially there were cell tower installations somewhere on the peaks, because every *caballero* she passed was on a cell phone and every *Rancho,* no matter how primitive, had a satellite dish. These were the descendants of the early *Californios,* Spanish adventurers who had found wives among the native population and created families in the New World, in Retreats of their own for two and a half centuries.

Becoming more nervous about her journey into the rugged canyon, and realizing that there were probably no *taller de llantas* where she was headed, Regina hoped that she wouldn't have to change a tire on her own?

Relieved to finally arrive at the Buddhist Retreat Center without any problems, she was welcomed by Lama Norbu's helpful disciples, thankful to find herself in such an etherial landscape. Tilting her gaze to the sky, Regina felt sheer wonder at the naked pinnacle thrust into the clouds so close above them. Ancient Fica trees had wound their smooth roots around giant boulders, forming a terraced landscape where she found Anni and the other woman gathering for the Retreat.

"Even though we have language barriers, we will be communicating on different levels." Anni was very convincing as she gathered her flock. "I have great Faith in music and dance, believing that we are all here to learn and grow, expanding our awareness through opening our hearts and loving each other and All that is."

What turned out to be an accidental coven, their ages from as old as 21 to as young as 83, the women would soon be embraced by the spirit of camaraderie. Most of the women spoke Spanish and the English speakers knew some Spanish, but with a little translation help from Anni, they were all soon comfortable with the language of smiles and laughter.

"On a practical everyday level, the tremendous help from my friends, their support and enthusiasm and especially cooking skills, are indispensable in all that I offer." Anni was introducing a graceful swan of a woman, Marvelous Marva, who was preparing a vegetarian meal that they would soon be sharing around tables set up in a rustic outdoor kitchen area.

A fire had been organized for moonrise. Huddling together close to the flames created an intimacy that kept away the cold of the night. Even with her limited Spanish, Regina managed to gain an appreciation for the essential oils that Ester had brought with her from *Michaocan*. She experienced compassion for one woman's fight with cancer, and another woman's disappointment with a child. Challenges and adventure: At eighty three, the oldest among them had a boyfriend thirty-five years younger than herself.

Having stayed up late into the night sharing stories around the fire under an almost full moon - *The Worm Moon* - the pilgrims were a little spaced as they gathered for pre-dawn meditation; everyone that is, except Anni.

"Spiritual practice brings consciousness and clarity to life" she explained brightly, leading them through some energy practices. "Let us embrace the Universe."

Dawn is a spiritual event for all beings and the soft hooting of a late retiring owl blended with the joy of morning bird song, as the avians among them prepared to take flight. Crowned by a majestic *palapa*, it was a scenic point in every dimension.

"Get comfortable and ground yourself between heaven and Earth" Anni directed. "Reach up and become a chalice, then bring the energy back to your heart, saying: *I open my heart to the great Divine.*" With palms facing up and arms spread expansively, Anni esoterically gathered an energy sphere between her palms.

"Bring the energy back to the heart and recite: *I receive a shower of blessings.*" The abstract became energy as they connected with the blessings.

"Now lay in a squashed frog posture of complete openness: *I invite my soul into my body.*" Closing her eyes in surrender, Regina was met by the voices of doves.

"Sit up into Happy Buddha Pose, soles of feet touching earth. With palms resting on top of your head, facing upward, swallow, allowing the energy to settle: *I fill my body with vitality.*"

"Bringing our hands down into meditation pose: *I dedicate my practice to all sentient beings.*"

Touched by a sun beam, the edges of the sheer rock formations balanced above them lit up. Anni then led her group through a series of energizing Chi Kung postures, encouraging them to "*Be here now.*" Stretching their limbs and opening their hearts, they reached a healing place just as the sun crested over the mountain horizon before rushing down the canyon walls to bring light to the meditation.

Changing into colorful clothing after breakfast, the group returned to find Anni setting up a sound system under the shade of the palapa. Accompanied by the simple steps that she taught them, they began dancing to traditional folk music from around the world, turning their circle into a rainbow of swirling color. Surrounded by the grandeur of a *Sierra* morning, the music and dances brought them to Peru, to India, to the British Isles, telling their stories through movement and gesture refined through history, touching the hearts of the dancers with both passion and respect for the creativity of the human spirit. Their focus was on the joy of dancing with new friends. Dancing through love, prancing through pain, swaying with disappointment and thrilling to melodies of happiness. Regina was thankful, also recognizing signs of gratitude among the other dancers. It was healing therapy for themselves and therefore for the Earth itself.

Pausing to rest at mid-day, Marva's lunch was another delicious work of art.

When they returned to the big *palapa,* Anni had laid out a project designed for individual creativity. Supplying each woman with a small clay container, they made selections from natural elements organized in little piles around the *palapa.* Intuitively gathering from the collection of materials, they each assembled personal totems. Regina selected pieces of healing amethyst to nestle in coral sand, as well as various pods and seeds that symbolized life cycles for her. Anni let the mountain sounds of bird song compliment her vast musical collection, while they completed their inner journey. After bundling their totems in colorful bandanas, Anni suggested they take some time to rest, instructing them to return wearing white, for an early dinner.

Small guest cottages were scattered along the ridge top retreat space and as roommates, Marva and Regina followed the path to their casita discussing their shared love for quilting, when the sound of low chanting caused them to pause at an open doorway. Peeking through the portal, they recognized the on-screen image of Lama Norbu, leading his *Baja* disciples in guided meditation from somewhere else in the world! Having naively mistaken the solitude of the retreat center as primitive, it was enlightening for them to see the Buddhist community creatively adapting elements of modern technology to stay spiritually connected with their teacher.

"Dance is a metaphor," Anni explained, "to flow with all that happens, to trust and know that all is well in this ever-changing Divine Plan." Surrounded by moonlit mountain-scape, the women were ready to believe.

The effect of dancing with lit candles was primordial. White cloth swirling, the Circle Dancers transformed into a whirlwind of spirit moths, each raising their light in tribute to the world around them. Transforming into moths was retreat, as each woman immersed herself in the rich experience that they were sharing. Suspending everyday realities made that place on the Tropic of Cancer free of sickness, free of tension and free from petty conflict, at least for the moment. Magnetically flowing in the spirit of new friendship, Regina had stopped thinking about

America's political stalemate. Trailing an actual entourage of moths to dance with the Divine, together they were captive to the light.

"There is so much light in the ordinary. When we connect to the miracle of every precious moment, the light shines forth and the more light that we experience, the more light that exists!"

With a toss of her moonlit curls, Anni picked up the pace of the next dance, a Hungarian Rhapsody, sending her group into a vortex of energy until they were vitalized to the core.

"We are spreading the light! Breathe with it. This is a healing ceremony for the Earth!" Anni had brought them to a pinnacle.

Soaked in moonlight, in awe of being part of something so beautiful, the women spiritually became One with the magic.

By the third day of the Retreat, morning meditation had become a cherished place to be. Greeting the light together was a bonding routine that they had quickly come to treasure. Then during breakfast, Anni explained that they would dance for a while longer and then she would be guiding them to another special place.

"Last night we felt the magic, and now I want you to feel the mystery."

The dogs that joined them from the ranchos located along the trail into the ravine were on good behavior, thankful for any gratuitous attention bestowed upon them. Taking the lead, they seemed to know where they were going.

A monumental Scenic Point, the stone monolith that greeted them was as tall and wide as a two story building. Obliquely similar to the shape of an iconic 80's plastic-fantastic Apple computer console, they also noticed that they were not the first pilgrims to visit. The giant boulder was layered on every surface with graffiti. Competing for space at ground level, the contemporary spray-painted messages covering its vertical surfaces gradually morphed into a multitude of handprints reaching to the heights, layers of greetings from predecessors. Channeling awe across time and place, palms from history saluted them from across the centuries. With early afternoon clouds drifting around the pinnacle that had birthed it, cosmic connections could be felt in every direction.

"I wonder if anybody saw that coming?" Marveling at the mystery, Marva directed their gaze upwards to the naked peak above and tried to imagine the force of Nature that had dislodged such a giant from its pedestal, to wedge itself so deeply into the ravine. The mountain peak had been a victim of gravity, but there was a sense of something else. Metaphorically comparing

Lama Norbu's disciples gathering before their computer screen to meditate with their teacher in real time across an ocean, Regina saw parallels with Anni's gathering.

Drawn to the mystery of a Rock of Ages, the women gathered in meditation on boulders strewn around the magnetic energy of the icon like planets in a solar system. Study of the textural composition of the stone and its geological characteristics, revealed sedimentary layers intrinsic to a place on the edge of time. The surface was worn smooth from the elements, touched by small sized and bigger palms, noticing that one hand was missing two fingers.

In a spirit of alliance, many of the women impulsively dipped their hands into the dancing rivulet flowing around the icon, pressing dripping palms onto the monolith, aligning with the prints of those who had been there before, watching their watery presence penetrate the warm stone.

"California!" Regina called out to the mystery. "We're still dancing on the edge of the world."

Seeds of Change

Gabriel Howearth was enthusiastic as he burst through the kitchen door. Regina had stopped by his *Buena Fortuna* Farm earlier that day to let him know that Bob Grunnet, a friend and a farmer from Camp Joy Garden in *Alta California* would be in town for a few days. Bob was really looking forward to a chance to talk with Gabriel about farming in the tropics and they connected like old friends, even though they were meeting for the first time.

The conversation soon delved into the chronology of the modern organic food movement that had begun in the 1960's. Gabriel had known the botanist Louie Sasso and through him had been inspired by Alan Chadwick, the biodynamic English horticulturist who had developed a philosophy for growing food sustainably. Teaching at the University of California Santa Cruz from 1967 to 1973, Alan and his devoted apprentices had created a showcase garden based on composting, the rhythms of nature and the role of the garden in human culture, important information in an evolving age of factory farms and engineered food. Evidently, he had been a formative influence for both of them, inspiring them to further the developing counter culture practices.

Bob had migrated to Camp Joy Garden in the Santa Cruz Mountains in 1972. Designed with a permaculture perspective by Alan Chadwick and a team of followers, including Beth and Jim Nelson, during his tenure at the nearby University, Camp Joy community farm provided valuable apprenticeships to students from all over the world, helping to spread the knowledge of organic farming during a time when "MonSatan", as Gabriel preferred to call the mega chemical company, was trying to change all the rules.

Gabriel was one of the founders of SEEDS OF CHANGE, the first organic seed company in the U.S.A. He was also one of the founders of the *Bioneers Conference,* an annual Alta California event developed to share knowledge and information about sustainable living. Through those connections he had traveled and lectured extensively, collecting seeds from around the world, spreading the knowledge of organic methods and especially about the importance of secure sources of organic seeds. Maintaining a sustainable system on a human scale, his *Buena Fortuna* Farm, the Good Fortune Coevolutionary Botanical Garden perched on the edge of the Tropic of Cancer, had become a genealogical seed bank and training center to supply seeds to an expanding worldwide market. During that time Gabriel had strongly influenced the local farming community to go organic, encouraging them as they formed local organic cooperatives, growing specialty produce for northern markets.

A torrent of information was flying between them and novices like Regina and Reggie could only try to pay attention. As the reality of feeding the world was becoming unsustainable in the twenty-first century, these were horticulturists who were helping to plant the seeds of sustainability that were challenging big agribusiness. Chris Hobbs, Dana Almond, Doug Guzman, Peter Dukish, Renee Shepherd, Kenny Ausulel all seemed to be mutual friends or acquaintances, all *bioneers* in a worldwide organic food movement.

Describing an Agricultural Conference of American Nations meeting in Cuba where he had made a presentation concerning the safety of seed stock, Gabriel shared an amazing episode about Fidel Castro, the notorious Cuban President. Castro had been so interested in his presentation that he had later arranged for a private meeting with him to learn more and it sounded like Fidel had made the most of the opportunity.

"I was really impressed with the quality of questions that he was bringing up for discussion." Gabriel was describing an amazing experience. "He was obviously concerned for the safety of his people and their reliance on secure sources of seeds. It's a wise leader that knows..." Gabriel paused then, his kinky hair electrified, to repeat a quote by Allen Watts: "Without seeds, there is no harvest."

"Was there a representative from the U.S.A. at the conference?" The question had to be asked.

"Of course not. That would be consorting with the enemy!" he mocked sarcastically. "Meanwhile, Cuba is the leading edge of the Organic Farming Movement while the U.S.A. is consorting with MonSatan!"

His icy blue eyes were shooting sparks before he paused to laugh at their perplexed expressions, going on to remind them about an upcoming yoga retreat in the nearby village of *Buena Vista*.

"Hey, don't worry, be happy! Oh, I know that's been said before, but we need to keep reminding each other. That's what Lama Norbu will tell you at the retreat next weekend. Meanwhile, come for the garden tour tomorrow. *Buena Fortuna* is a showcase for botanical specimens from all over the world. Ten o'clock. Be there *amigos!*" he called over his shoulder as he headed back to the farm.

Stepping over the cattle guard into *Buena Fortuna* was like waking into a dream. Leaving behind the naked winter desert, a cool veil of green welcomed them to a tropical paradise. The shade from a rudimentary *Palo de Arco* stick shelter crawling with flowering vines made a welcoming hospitality zone. A Farmers Market was already under way as Gabriel's culturally fashionable wife Kitzia was arranging freshly harvested fruits and veggies from the garden into an amazing cornucopia surrounded by bouquets of fresh flowers. Allured by her beauty, she was a magnet for the visitors who were already assembling for the tour.

"Eighty percent of plant diversity resides in the tropics" Gabriel began lecturing as Bob and his *amigos* joined the group, "and of the 10,000 species of plants growing in the *California Floristic Provence*, 47% of the plant diversity is here in *Baja*

California. Having two seasons a year in the dry tropics speeds up plant genetics, enabling us to quickly develop breeding lines. Our goal is to develop seeds that are drought tolerant and low maintenance. We have a seed arc of over 3700 plant species here in the garden, including edible, medicinal, sacred and native plants." Gabriel's rapid fire delivery continued as he led the group into the shady paths of his botanical garden.

"We practice Polyculture here. Notice how we've incorporated native plants and perennials that attract pollinators and help to fix nitrogen in the soil with integrated seasonal crops." Pausing for a moment to let his group grasp this important concept, Gabriel got right to the point: "Permaculture farming is holistic and respects the relationships between all the parts."

Laid out in related family classifications of plants that he had collected from around the world, the tour first passed through groves of citrus from the order *Sapindales*. Guavas from order *Myrtales* and *Neems* from order *Rutales* were flowering exotically. Inviting them to touch and smell as they explored, he described his goal of creating a living genealogy of plants there at *Buena Fortuna* Farm.

"Did you know that there are 6000 types of mangos in the world?" Gabriel slung out information in big chunks while he led them further, past dense clusters of banana and bamboo, eventually bringing them to the main living structure in the center of the garden. The enchanting brick building that towered into the canopy, was circled by a perimeter of *palapa* roofing hung with broad baskets of drying seeds.

"*Baja California Sur* is the furthest north dry tropic in the world. Because it's so dry here, it makes it a good place for seed saving."

Intricate stick furniture and woven fiber hammocks along with an assortment of musical instruments completed the allusion of a counterculture paradise. It was a fantastic photo opportunity, but Gabriel didn't linger.

"Plants really respond to music" he stated without elaboration, leading them into the area of desert plants.

Of the three hundred varieties of aloe in the world, Gabriel had collected two hundred specimens. Confirmed by archeological digs in the Southwest United States, he had reintroduced *quinoa* and *amaranth* to North America, and now supplied those seeds to a worldwide market.

Plantings in the shapes of geometric symbols spread throughout the garden, were beautiful reminders of sacred associations with plants. Pausing to admire a brilliant bed laid out in the form of a Sun Ray, Regina finally had to ask about the huge diversity of plants that had been brought together from all over the world.

"Do you have concerns Gabriel, that you might inadvertently contaminate native plants by bringing in all these non-natives?" It was a question that she had not thought of all by herself.

Gabriel's answer was swift.

"In a world of shrinking bio-diversity, we have to protect our plant sources. If anything happens in one area, there need to be viable plants elsewhere to replant. It's all about preservation. For instance, a few years ago I was asked to reintroduce some plants back into Madagascar."

Gabriel then went on to describe other plant saving techniques, such as placing seeds within pyramids, which he had helped to do in locations in Central and South American countries.

Continuing to the composting area, Gabriel was emphatic about the benefits of heavy composting for desert farming. Describing a vigorous process of Pedogenesis, he proudly turned over the compost pile to reveal worms and insects that were so vital to the creation of soil. After digging around for a bit with the bugs, the tour wound it's way back through a nursery area with potted plants for sale, coming out where they had begun. Kitzia and a helper were there under the flowering gazebo preparing cups of water and fresh juices and slicing open a sumptuous ripe papaya for the returning visitors to snack on before sitting down for the organic brunch that was included after the tour.

The farm was only eleven acres, but the tour had covered almost every corner and they were all thirsty. As she reached for a cup, Regina experienced a dawning sense of disbelief. Emerging like a mirage from behind a massive basket of citrus, the face of Kitzia's helper surprisingly came into clear focus and suddenly they were being introduced to a well-known counter culture heroine: It was Julia Butterfly.

Julia 'Butterfly 'Hill had earned notoriety as a fearless conservationist by camping out in the branches of an ancient northern California redwood tree for over two years to keep it from being felled in a Humboldt clear cut. She had been a tireless voice for the environmental movement ever since and in the process had inspired a legion of followers, her courage establishing a strong movement for old growth protection and earning her a reputation as a mighty warrior.

"Purpose, passion and power." The deep voice of Julia Butterfly was emphatic as she described her developing philosophy. "If a person can identify a clear purpose and pursue it with passion, it will empower them."

There was darkness between them, but they didn't need to see her to hear the conviction in her words. Sirius was high in the sky and the blackened silhouettes of the surrounding palms were starkly visible against the starry sky. Leaning back against slippery boulders, they were soaking in the warmth of a steaming pool of natural spring water seeping from the massive wall of granite towering above them in the darkness.

It was Gabriel's birthday, and Kitzia had loaded up the children and a small posse of friends along with baskets of fresh food from the garden and led them into the mountains of the Biosphere above *Santiago* to celebrate together in the hot springs. She had also brought special cake. Lighting candles as they waited for the moonrise, Regina could hardly believe that she was soaking under the stars with botanical superheroes.

"*Que pasa,* Julia" Reggie called out from the hot spot over by the base of the giant boulder wall. "Did I hear that your father was a preacher?"

"Yes" she admitted honestly, "and ironically it seems that I've taken the show on the road. We're even thinking about a place in the tropics where we could farm and research in the winter. The rest of our time would be in Ashland where our foundation is centered."

"I personally believe that food can be grown anywhere on the planet. So now we're here to learn about farming in tropical deserts." The voice joining the conversation belonged to Julia's partner, Chris.

"The paradox of our situation though, is that now we are getting tired" Julia confessed honestly. "We don't want to be traveling so much. It's too hard on us and too hard on the earth. We want to become locavores, focusing our energies locally, eating locally and eating seasonally."

There was a flurry of excited chatter as they discussed Julia's reasoning.

"That's a new word for me" Regina admitted candidly, sensing that she would be learning something valuable.

"It was a Webster's Word of the Year. Basically, it refers to a person that focuses their energy locally and seasonally."

Chris was measuring the nutritional content of food and his research had led him to believe that food could be grown anywhere in the world under protected growing conditions and with the help of soil supplementation. He was dedicating his life to that pursuit. Going on to describe his work on soil enrichment, Chris and Gabriel began a reasoning session about the vital importance of Mycorrhizae association between fungi and bacteria in soil creation. Somewhere up the canyon the call and answer of coyotes on the hunt reminded them that they were not alone.

"Many foods travel" Julia thoughtfully reflected, passing her plate over for another slice of cake. "Currently, one plate of food might collectively travel 25,000 miles to be consumed. An olive may have been transported 6,000 miles to your plate!" Julia was sounding like her father's daughter as she expounded on her developing theory and purpose. She and Chris were organizing.

"The *Circle of Life Foundation* is our way of activating people to live in a way that honors the diversity and interdependence of all life" she declared, going on to elaborate.

"The trouble with big charity organizations is the top heavy bureaucracy. Smaller more focused organizations like ours, direct a larger percentage of donations to the beneficiaries. For instance, our Pollination Project gives small seed grants for individual Change Makers. Together those small projects are the ones that will be creating the big changes that the Earth needs."

"That's a big idea with clear purpose." It was a point to meditate on while Kitzia suckled her baby to sleep before quietly continuing.

"Now you have the passion, and it's given you the power, Julia."

"You are all planting seeds of change" Regina insisted. "Your agricultural projects will lead us towards a more sustainable Earth."

Prophetically, the narrow canyon was suddenly lit by the emergence of a waning moon over the rocky horizon, casting magic onto the monumental granite boulders surrounding them. Worn smooth by generations of flowing water, subtle shadowing morphed them into reclining figures, luminous ancestors suspended in stone. Moon reflections on the water created aboriginal hieroglyphics, steamy messages from the spiritual world.

The visitors humbly gathered their things while the coyotes continued their yips and howls further up the canyon, channeling their own ancestors. Following the worn path, Kitzia led her pack back up the hillside toward the little *rancho* where they had left their transportation back to civilization. Winding through the shadowy maze of well-defined campsites surrounding the spring, signs of their predecessors were everywhere. Pausing at the rock circle under the gigantic Fica tree that dominated the area, the *amigos* romantically embraced the timelessness of the place. Then as now, this was a place of communion, a gathering place through antiquity.

Much like a seed, they felt the spirit of the land all around them.

Learning to Fly

Visitors are welcome occasions to share the natural wonders of life on the East Cape. Walks along the sparkling shoreline could become extraordinary excursions into wonderland, especially to a six years old who was positive that each speck of mica on the beach was real gold. Every glimpse of a sea creature scurrying into the obscurity of deeper water evoked a gleeful response, although a ten second glimpse through a diving mask was the extent of her underwater bravery. The realization that black and yellow stripped fish were circling her ankles convinced her that searching for seashells with her grandparents on the beach was a preferable option to deep water adventure. While her more adventurous parents immersed themselves in a snorkeling safari, an expanding collection of seashells became her treasure. She thought it was so funny when some cows settled into the shade of a nearby *palapa*.

After a while, *Isla Cerralvo* disappeared from the northern horizon into haze and Regina knew that the wind would soon be coming up. She had been spending winters on the East Cape long enough to recognize that local signal of transition. The playful rolling swells that her family had been enjoying that morning would soon become churning waves. Signaling that it was time to take that last swim, she began to gather up the belongings strewn around the palapa.

Scattering a flock of Snowy Plovers that had been running along the frothy wave line, Dahlia splashed along behind them, mimicking their abrupt flight. Right at that very moment, a formation of Pelicans skimmed directly over her, en-route to a destination of their own. Following their flight out to Sea, Regina was the only one to notice the breaching of a whale close to the wind line, starting to be visible just below the horizon to the north.

The mass of nature was warping ordinary time under a sky of soaring birds as Regina and her grand daughter made their way between tawny dunes along the sweeping shoreline. The previously clear blue sky was now seething with puffy strands of cirrocumulus clouds driven by a fierce wind from the north that had forced the rest of the family back to the *casa* for *siesta* time. Unfazed, the youngest among them had convinced her *Abuela,* her grandmother to stay for more time in the elements. The fleeting charm of infancy was fading as she opened her mind for the natural world to pour in.

Sheltered from the sun and the wind, they settled in near a tenacious patch of Tamarisk overlooking the estuary to the south. Drooping with fluffy pink blossoms and swarming with honeybees, the fragrance was a sweet perfume. Along with the peaceful drone of bees gathering pollen from the delicate pink blossoms surrounding them, the afternoon pulsed with life. Respectfully watching the peaceful panorama around them, their presence soon blended into the landscape. A surprised Roadrunner paused close by them before disappearing into the bushes.

The estuary had a lot more activity than a first impression might have suggested. White butterflies and iridescent red dragonflies flitted below the wind line behind the dunes as they carried on their migrant lives amidst the flowering foliage. Ducks and coots sifted through the muddy edges of the lagoon, hoping to get lucky. A pair of soaring Frigate birds were mirrored in the watery reflection of sky. The trill of Osprey riding high on the wind, blended with the returning tide to churn out a relentless rhythm.

Thanks to John Spencer, the local "Baja Birder", Grandmother was able to identify many bird species for Dahlia. Having lived in the area for decades, he was the local authority for bird identification on the East Cape. Always making himself available for bird watching excursions along the shore or out on the desert, his wry wit and depth of knowledge was a treasure that he had enthusiastically shared with ornithologists from all around the world.

The little girl was the first to hear the bells and she was thrilled as the reflections on the water rippled with the arrival of a pair of mares. Knee deep in the murky water, they were casually munching the greenery growing along the banks, with their playful foals charging together through the rushes. Flushed from the undergrowth, a bevy of ducks created a whisper of wings as they abruptly fled to another muddy flat. Across a patch of tulles, a Blue Heron remained unperturbed, continuing its vigil for an afternoon snack.

More bells announced the arrival of the rest of the herd. Emerging from a nearby dune, a towering stallion posed on the ridge to appraise them. Evidently the sight of the interlopers didn't arouse much interest and after a careful inspection and a couple of snorts the stallion resumed his mission, leading the rest of his herd over to join their friends on the far side of the lagoon. Paying special attention to one mare, the stallion suddenly progressed from arousal to a mounting position, requiring a brief explanation from Grandmother. When they later disappeared from view, the human companions were left with the mystique of wild horses, even though Grandmother knew that the herd was probably headed back to their rancho for feeding time.

Earlier that afternoon Regina had vaguely noticed some sightseers parked on the beach road, pointing towards the lagoon from the windows of super-sized SUVs with tinted windows. Now appearing on the beach, holding on to their broad rimmed hats and each other, a troop of *gringos* were reverently following their leader straight into the wind, marching right down the beach toward them in tight formation.

They were dressed conspicuously in bright resort attire, and with closer inspection as they paraded close by, inappropriate shoes. With not a sign of acknowledgment, ignoring friendly greetings, seemingly oblivious of the beauty surrounding them, the tightly clustered group always deferred obediently to their leader. Waving around what looked like a big map, it was clear that he was the one with the vision. Scaring away the Blue Heron with his abrupt gestures, he was pointing this way and that like a vicar with a grand scheme. Directing their gaze towards the purple mountains on the southern horizon, then West toward Flat Top and finally circling back to the lagoon, a fair judgment seemed to suggest that this was a group of potential investors.

With a sinking heart Regina endured the presumption of their presence. The vultures were circling curiously as the head *honcho* pulled something from his backpack and the group parted to reveal the insult of an orange ribbon fluttering from a flowering bush alongside the lagoon.

"Orange alert!"

It was looking like this might be the beginning of another ugly chapter in the continuing conquest of *California*. She liked the color orange, but even the little girl realized that these orange ribbons weren't a part of sharing. Mexico's beaches are protected up to 40 meters from the high tide line and the wild life depends on that protection. This was a public beach and most people recognized that they needed to respect the space, but these people were different, acting with unspoken privilege.

Grandmother wanted to run back up the beach and shout an alert to the pelicans waiting on the shore for handouts from returning fishermen. She needed to warn the ducks! Maybe the gulls would cry the alarm? Instead, she was frozen in disbelief as more orange ribbons appeared along the line of dunes.

"Looks like these investors are listening to some big ideas." the elder lamented, thinking back on stories of the Conquest that had begun centuries earlier.

"Those people are modern *Conquistadores*" Grandmother explained to her young companion while they watched the returning spectacle march back down the beach towards them. "They're not even aware of this fragile environment. They might even be planning to develop this part of the coast for themselves..." Next to her, the child practiced flying, creating angels in the sand.

Regina stood up to quote an architectural hero, hoping that the philosophy of Frank Lloyd Wright might be able to shed a timely lesson.

"Respect for place is the best beginning for any architectural project. Don't make a mark on the land until you have spent a year watching the place." What they were witnessing was a complete disconnect from that philosophy, except the wind took her words, so only the granddaughter heard the advice.

Grandmother wanted to confront the speculators, but somehow, they weren't able to shed their cloak of invisibility as the gang trouped past them, deep in their own parallel reality, heading for the security of their SUVs.

Dust on the horizon finally confirmed the departure of the invaders as Grandmother began the charge. Leading them down the line of dunes, the young one soon got into the spirit, breathlessly racing to each offending ribbon and ripping it off the foliage with a squeal of satisfaction, before running back to Grandmother with her trophy. Under a tangerine sky, she could tell that she was making Grandmother happy.

Some people would accuse her of teaching vandalism. Others might even define their act as terrorism, but Grandmother wanted to be a revolutionary! In Mexico on a tourist visa, could she circulate a petition? Maybe she could reason with the *ejido* of the village? What would make a difference in an impoverished village dreaming of prosperity?

When the two comrades finally headed for home, the lights across the *Bahia* were twinkling to life below the purple silhouette of the *Sierra de la Laguna*. Practicing her new awareness, the little one was swooping ahead, arms widespread, skimming along the surf line towards a vista of fishing boats strewn across the sand like beached whales.

A local family was following a boil of fish along the surf ahead of them, the father tossing his net into the school, while mother and children ran along the shore behind him with buckets for the catch. Pausing with them to marvel at the squirming bucket of silvery fish, they all watched breathlessly as a returning fisherman ran the beach just in front of them, lifting his motor out of the water just in time to slide up safely beyond reach of the shoreline surge. Mostly Sierras and giant Yellowtail, the catch would be loaded onto pick-ups headed for *Cabo* markets. Scraps were tossed to a noisy hoard of beach scavengers. Gulls and Pelicans got very competitive as they noisily bickered over the spoils. Spreading out their nets for cleaning and repairs, the mood was jovial as the fishermen shared stories about their day on the Sea of Cortez while the lights on the shrimp boats were coming to life out on the *Bahia,* in preparation for night fishing.

Collecting a couple of fish to take back to *la casa,* the wind had finally taken a *siesta* as the daring duo, a generations apart, followed flocks of Egrets flying above them against a sky of mauve, heading inland to nest overnight. Under the sliver of a new moon hanging over the East Cape village where she spent her winters, Regina allowed herself to imagine that the estuary might have a tiny reprieve before the next assault, thankful for an intrepid grand-daughter and a brief illusion of victory.

Forgotten Relics

Tucked into the north end of the East Cape, *Los Barriles* is the epicenter of *Gringo-landia*. With predictable fierce wind patterns, the area is a magnet for thrill sports, especially attracting kite and wind surfers addicted to adrenaline. With the only bank between Los Cabos and La Paz, health clinics, grocery stores, bars and restaurant with live music and food options that include Italian Pizza to Pacific Sushi, curio shops, quad rentals and luxury accommodations, it is a popular destination point for an international population. Like many others in the *gringo* community, Reggie and Regina had many connections there.

Errands in *Barriles* often included tacos at *El Viejo*. Hidden by a shroud of colorful bougainvillea, a patio restaurant with plastic tables and chairs might not seem like a social vortex for the *gringo* community, but if you can find an available table, the *comidas* never disappoints. With the taco bar loaded with Mexican specialties, your taco is guaranteed to be a culinary work of art. Not just salsa and cabbage, heap your taco from multiple bowls of onion concoctions, fresh sliced cucumbers, spicy pickled carrots, peppers, Rajas - cooked poblano peppers in cream - and everyone's favorite, *guacamole*.

Sitting down with Regina at the last available table, Reggie couldn't help noticing the *gringo* returning to the table across from him with a mounded plate dripping with *salsa* and *guacamole*. It took a while, giving the waiter a chance to take their order and bring them drinks, but he eventually remembered where he had seen the man before. When the *hombre* had eventually finished his *comidas*, he leaned over to ask an eager question.

"Aren't you the Jazz musician that we saw playing at the San *Antonio Historic Home Tour*? You really turned me on to Jazz. I've even taken some lessons." It turned out to be a pivotal musical link for them all.

Sloping his gaze over the rim of his glasses, the Jazzman cautiously acknowledged the recognition, while his family turned curiously towards the interruption. They were Snowbirds from the state of Washington where he and his wife Dona Rainy lived on a boat in the Puget Sound. Their son was visiting from the home. It had been he that they'd seen playing in *San Antonio*. The oldest continuously populated civil community in all of *California*, the *Home Tour* had been a memorable experience, allowing the public to explore the interior of some of *California's* earliest colonial buildings. After Reggie heard him playing guitar in the parlor of one of the historic homes, he had been inspired to learn more about Jazz and was stoked to be able to now accept an invitation to get together for a jam.

While making those plans and discussing different musical influences, Regina and Rainy were making their own connections. A psychiatric nurse in Bellingham, she and Jazzman spent winters playing music and painting in *Rancho Verde*, a community in the mountains beyond *Los Barriles*. Eagerly listening to Rainy describe the adventures of life on the slopes of *Mt. Ballena,* Regina detected compelling details about one of Rainy's favorite hikes to "the Governor's Mansion."

"Established for mining, it was actually the very first non mission town in *California*" Rainy explained. "We've seen all kinds of relics from the old days on our hikes through the area."

Further explaining that their historian friend Russ Hyslop had told them that it was the site of an infamous historical community, Regina questioned her until she felt sure that it really was the *Santa Ana* of the legendary *Sacred Expedition.*

So close to the source of legend, Regina then explained her own curiosity about the Missions and *California* history, lingering sentimentally on Monterey family stories heard in her youth about Junipero Serra, the legendary figure now recognized as the Father of California.

Emotionally engaged and always up for a hike, Rainy volunteered to guide them to the old mining settlement, combining the plans that the musicians were making with Regina and Reggies lifelong odyssey exploring *California.*

After winding up the wide *Buenas Aries arroyo* above *Barriles* from the Sea of Cortez, the East Cape explorers cruised into the scenic tropical village of *San Bartolo,* a spring-fed oasis planted with huge old mango, citrus and avocado trees, tropical with date and coconut palms. Colorful shops and restaurants lined the *camino* advertising sweets. The enterprising women in the village have built an industry around jams and jellies made from those local fruits and remembering the Jazzman's appetite, Reggie was ready to stock up for the visit with their new friends in *Rancho Verde.*

Stopping at a *Dulceria Regionalis*, its entrance draped with bags of oranges, grapefruits and avocados, they discovered the preserved fruit specialties that the community is famous for. Displays of homemade sweets got Reggie really excited as he tried to make some choices. *Empanadas* filled with jellied mango and guayaba were soon stacked on the counter along with, bags of fresh fruit, *Burritos de Machaca* and golden cookies called *Galletas de Piloncillo*. The collection of old spurs displayed over the sales counter was also impressive. Passing on the mandatory cooler of Coca-Cola and an astounding display of chips, they weren't going to arrive empty handed.

Continuing to follow the *arroyo*, the *camino* led into a wide green valley, a radical departure from the usually dry sea level vistas of cactus that they were accustomed to seeing. *Rancho Verde* lay at the foot of the boulder studded flanks of *Mt. Ballena*. They didn't have to wonder about the iconography of that name: The gigantic monoliths of granite clearly did resemble the thrusting forms of whales.

Inching along behind slow moving cattle blocking the narrow tract through the *Rancho,* the welcoming faces of Rainy and Jazzman finally directed them into the driveway of *Casa Torote Mundo* and an up-close glimpse into an off the grid alternative community. Completely self-sustaining, their charming life style was powered by solar installations. They had developed their own gravity fed water system and the cool mountain breeze provided air conditioning. The visiting coastal dwellers were amazed by their host's ingenuity as they pointed out solar ovens and utilities all powered by the sun. Jazzman had also converted an old trailer house into a music room full of sound equipment that doubled as a guest house, but since they expected it to get cool in the evening, they decided to jam on the patio, closer to the kitchen fireplace. Discovering Rainy's soulful soprano made the groove complete as they played and dined under a sunset sky turning orange, simmering into red before fading into a canopy of stars. With the Milky Way sparkling above them, it was a poetic beginning for the Picante Jazz Cats.

"Holy shit!" The sound of breaking glass rudely woke Regina up when Reggie dropped his glass of water in the sink.

"To think that we were sleeping with that monster!" he shouted, A giant black scorpion had fled down the drain as Reggie was getting ready to brush his teeth. That incident got Regina up in a hurry.

Jazz Man already had the fire going when they joined their friends on the dining room patio and Rainy had hot coffee ready to go with the pastries from *San Bartolo*. It became a wake'n'bake morning for Regina who was still recovering from the scorpion scare, but Reggie and Jazzman didn't miss a beat. Ready to create a musical tradition, they dove back into jazz right after coffee, continuing from where they had left off the night before, while their partners planned the excursion to Santa Ana.

Sensing Regina's hopeful expectations, Rainy tried to keep things in perspective with a description of what she remembered from her last visit.

"I especially remember getting thirsty and hungry, so I'm packing a picnic this time" she counseled, already bagging up some of the ripe avocados from *San Bartolo*. Her contagious laugh was a reminder of the playful chatter of gulls.

'Oh, perfect..." Regina responded in a distracted sort of way, while filling their water bottles from a distillery that Jazz had installed. "....and how about those *piloncillos?"* But too late. A Cookie Monster had already finished them off when they weren't looking.

"Hope you won't be disappointed, Sweetie" Rainy cautioned. "When the silver ore was depleted, mining activity shifted to *San Antonio*. You'll find only overgrown relics now."

After a short drive down the slope from *Rancho Verde* they turned to follow the dry riverbed of *Agua Blanca*. Pausing there to admire the scenic vista, a panorama of cactus formed a hazy plain swooping to meet the sea channel between *Isla Ceralvo* and the *Surgidero*.

"The landing place where Spanish ships would have delivered early travelers from the Sea of Cortez. They would have walked up the riverbed from there" Jazzman explained.   Turning up the *arroyo* from there, it was exciting to realize that they were following the historical route to *Santa Ana*. Winding southwest around the base of *Mt. Ballena*, they drove deeper into the *Sierra de las Lagunas* mountains following the ever more brilliant *Agua Blanca* into a seemingly parallel reality - at least that's how it felt to Regina. When they passed a sign identifying *Rancho Santa Ana*, the enormity of the adventure started emerging for her. Finally reaching a towering old oak, they parked their vehicle in the shade and Rainy explained that they would be walking from there.

"The caravans to *Todos Santos* continued west from here, but I think I remember...." Pausing to speculate, it seemed that mystery lingered a little for them all. "The Governor's mansion is along the *arroyo* in this other direction" she decided.

Reggie and Regina had been romantically thinking of themselves as crusaders following courageous footsteps, but instead found themselves dodging cow pies, following the footsteps of a free-range cattle trail. With prints from many wild animals criss crossing through the dazzling white sand around them, every shadow through the landscape of oaks and boulders was suspect.

When bubbly airborne puffs began to drift toward them, it seemed as if the supernatural was going to make an appearance. Rounding a sharp corner, they discovered towering cottonwoods shedding clouds of filament in a bizarre welcome to *Santa Ana*.

"Judging by the size of these trees, they've been around for a long time." Reggie was impressed. With trunks at least four feet in diameter soaring majestically above them, they might have had stories to tell.

Stunned by anticipation, the explorers watched as a sudden gust erupted to spin particles from the tree into a ghostly cloud. Swirling into an area of archeological relics, the twister swept up wide stairs cut into the embankment leading to a stately old mansion overlooking the broad curve of the *arroyo*. Touched by the significance of their discovery, their lives had intrinsically become connected to what had begun there two and a half centuries earlier. Perched on the radiant edge of the *Agua Blanca,* it was among these ruins that the *Padre Presidente,* Junipero Serra, the explorer Gasper de Portola and the Spanish King's Viceroy, Jose de Galvaz, an epic trio of visionaries, had so portentously made their fateful plans for *California*: The *Sacred Expedition* that had led them to Monterey.

From the perspective of their own 21st Century odyssey, it was momentous for Reggie and Regina to realize how the legends of childhood had finally manifest at this place of ruins. Counting the eroded pillars on the patio of the collapsing but still impressive mansion, mystery lingered in every shadow. Peering into a partially blocked doorway, they discovered most of the ceiling collapsed onto the floor of a grand central room, blocking access to other side rooms. Plants and vines were growing out of the floor and walls in a way that had in a sense kept the dream alive.

"And we're still dreaming!" Regina loudly informed any loitering spirits.

Further exploration of the abandoned mining community revealed crumbling mining shafts and ruins of water driven ore mills and even a beehive smelting oven that still looked serviceable.

"Find me some clay!" Reggie was ready to fire it up, but hesitant to explore too deeply after Regina's reminder of his recent scorpion episode.

"There is a lot of clay deposited in these valleys" Jazzman informed them. "Further toward La Paz, just beyond the Cactus Sanctuary, there's a village that specializes in things made out of clay. We'll visit there in the future."

But at the time, full immersion in Santa Ana was enough. A few steps later Regina abruptly felt herself slipping, barely managing to keep from falling into an overgrown hole in the ground. Peering into the deep pit, she wondered if it might have been an overgrown latrine? Located on a slight rise not far from the mansion, it seemed like a logical possibility to Regina.

"I doubt that they had indoor plumbing in those days." she speculated.

From that vantage point slightly above low foliage, the view of *Santa Ana* revealed a small valley of grassy chaparral typical of the Sierra Lagunas at that elevation, surrounded by slopes covered with an Oak-Pinon woodland. If there had been a plan for the city, it was no longer visible. A few taller trees followed the white ribbon of river. Random cottonseed twisters continued to haunt the landscape as they explored the old mining enterprise looking for evidence of it's historical past. Even a pile of rocks were cause for conjecture. It was challenging to realize that such a grand enterprise could have vanished so completely. Trying to imagine the lives of those early entrepreneurs, Regina remembered that Rainy had told her that before long, they had moved to *San Antonio.*

"We were lucky to have been able to visit the interiors of those historic homes on the Tour. Because we met you there, those spirits were able to lead us here..." she explained cryptically to her new friends, "...to the very beginning of *Nuevo California.*"

The exploration wasn't going much further than that as the heat of mid-day rippled across *Mt. Ballena,* continuing the illusion of breaching whales on the horizon. Settling themselves in the shade of the mansion patio overlooking the brilliant path of dry river sand, counting the crumbling pillars seemed mandatory. Propping themselves against the wall of what they suspected might have once been the kitchen, fantasizing the menu of historical lunches while Rainy unpacked their picnic. A string of long horned cattle, stoically walking by in single file, stirred up more fluffy whirlwinds to dance before them. The ghostly forms were putting on quite the show when a pair of Scrub Jays cavorting through some nearby oaks flushed out a family of Quail. Imbedded in nature, the spirit of the place was manifesting around them in so many ways.

"The menu had to have included beef" Reggie cynically joked while Dona Rainy handed him a cheese sandwich bulging with avocado.

"Ancestors of the *Chinampo* breed introduced from Spain by the early missionaries" Jazzman clarified stoically.

"I know it's Physics that form these whirlwinds up the *arroyo...* then is it Quantum Physics that turn them into luminous beings?" Regina was still working on her hypothesis, going on to wonder how the relics of *Santa Ana* had remained so obscure.

"The origin of a new destiny for *California,* now a playground for ghosts?" Rainy handed her a cup of lemonade.

'Stay hydrated" she advised, wondering if her friend was becoming illusional.

Charlie, the dog that had been walking with them that afternoon, found the dead carcass of a dove to play with, throwing it around while vultures began seeping from the purple horizon to circle above them curiously.

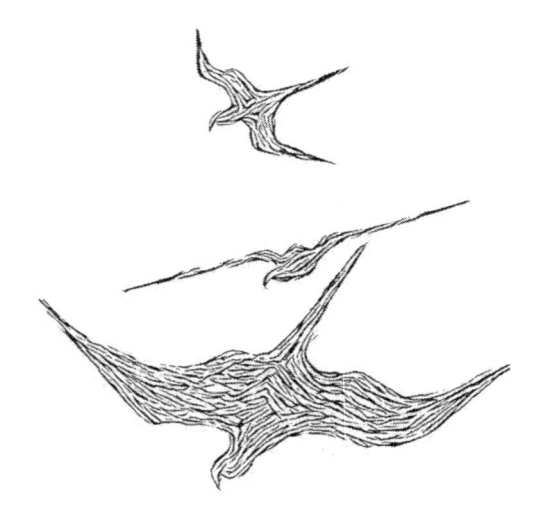

The Two Timers

The *Two Timers* were trying to keep a steady rhythm despite the spectacle created by their wanna-be drummer, epically pounding away on his shiny new drum set in complete disregard for whichever song they may have just agreed to play.

"This guy must be on speed" the *gringo* musicians had declared after their first practice. That's when *Dos Dannys* had decided that for this gig, they would be the *Two Timers*.

"...cause there just isn't going to be a third time with this character!"

"Oh yeeeah, you really got me goin'... I can't sleep at niiiight..." the drummer screamed out in his nervy version of a

Hollywood rock star. With his hairy chest protruding from an unbuttoned Hawaiian shirt and his bleached-out surfer locks hanging over his wrap-around sunglasses, he almost looked the part... but not quite. Whether it was called "Bay Watch" or "Surf Grunge" it was impossible to ignore the fact that Skip was way off beat.

The startled audience of agents and speculators there to survey the potential "Cactus Point Development" hadn't expected to be held hostage to their host's Hard Rock delusions. Understandably, most of the audience was getting up to take a walk as the tangle of competing beats came close to meltdown. Regina and Yolanda, along with some flagrant groupies from the village, were there to support their *amigos,*

"This is only the second time that we've played together" Skip brazenly acknowledged, "and if it's bad... then it's just too bad!" An outburst of fury on the cymbals was evidently meant to convince the audience that he really meant it.

"Oh yeeeeah, I can't sleep at niiiiiight, I can't sleep at niiiight!"

Ugly rumors about development of the environmentally sensitive area along the East Cape had been circulating the village and curious, they were there on a fact-finding mission, hoping to discover some truth about the project along the majestic shore of the Sea of Cortez. A complimentary lunch had also been a lure.

Surveying the sparkling panorama of sand and sea alongside the party area, Regina and her friends realized that a big chunk of the environment wouldn't be getting a second chance. Bulldozers and graders had already sliced up the low-lying desert area around them, leading the Cactus Development into phases I through IV minus a lot of cacti, with further development on the drawing board.

"Desert plants take a long time to grow" Ruth explained. "Consider that a Cardon cactus grows only 2.5 cm in a good year..." A retired teacher in her other life in Santa Barbara and with thirty years of experiences on the East Cape, she was an authority figure among the seasonal ex-pats.

Directing their gaze back toward hillsides covered with massive Cardon, ribbed; columnar branches were easily 20 meters high.

"Do the math, *amigos*!" she instructed, her ice blue eyes piercing with conviction. "It's taken centuries for these giant forests to dominate the desert and many animals depend on them for seeds and nesting. It's unbelievable that Mexico would consider this development" she sputtered. "This, this, **this** is destruction!" Ruth was appalled at the discovery.

So far only a couple of hardy souls had braved the elements to stake their claims on Cactus Point, but with the Baby Boomers on their way, even with factors like the need for a source of reliable water and inevitable hurricanes, it didn't leave much space for optimism. Along with those considerations a creepy recognition as to the true motives of the drummer was seeping into Regina's consciousness. She had seen Skip before, leading potential investors along the beach in their own village.

She was imagining the beautiful infinity pool filled with sand, when the turbulence of the *Two Timers* finally subsided. Then it was a welcome relief for them to hear the mellow harmonies of *Dos Dannys* drifting out over the shimmering Sea of Cortez, while the drummer headed over to cut off the stampede to the busses.

"So, we hear that you are also involved in the project at *La Riviera*? There's rumor about a marina." the villagers quizzed Skip as he later made the rounds. Being seasonal locals, the whole table was curious about the recently installed barbed wire fence blocking access to the local beach. He didn't want to talk about it, condescending as he consistently blocked vital questions about laws involving beach access and habitat.

" Hey, no more questions about the marina. This is a party for Cactus Estates. Why not just go stuff your face and drink another margarita? Have some fun!" he joked crudely, pointing toward the gourmet buffet table set up on the far side of the pool, obnoxiously reminding them that everything was complimentary.

"**Everybody have another margarita!**" With his arms waving in wild salutation, even a deaf person might have been suspicious.

Hoping that another round of refreshments might soften the edges of the situation, the village *amigos* obediently marched back to the bar for another *margarita*. Ordering from a broad selection of top *tequilas*, every label guaranteed *"Pura Agave"*. In the States they would have been wine tasting, but in Mexico it was *tequila* tasting. More or less the same, they all understood that it was a standard ruse to juice up potential clients.

Mingling with the tourists that had been bused in from *Cabo*, an undercurrent of skepticism soon made the locals realize that the speculators weren't as vulnerable as they might have imagined. Many had come to sight-see, but some were actually thoughtful investors.

"I heard that there's no water available to this development" confided one elderly couple before they were interrupted by the loco drummer.

"**No water!**" Skip had overheard them. "What does that look like in the swimming pool, stupid? Just kidding, but don't go spreading false rumors about things you don't know about!"

"He needs an attitude adjustment if he realistically expects to attract any investors" Yolanda counseled the elders as they recoiled from the unexpected verbal abuse.

Regina wanted to get in his face about the cycles of severe drought that they periodically endured in *Baja California.* They knew that water was being trucked into Cactus Point, but at the same time it was hard to ignore the infinity pool disappearing into the horizon.

"Did I see you looking around at the model across from the office?" Blatantly changing the subject from water, Skip was getting confrontational before she could ask the question.

"I live across from there, but hey, don't even think about looking in there, cause it's none of your business!" He couldn't seem to help his rude outbursts.

Leaving them gaping in disbelief he stomped off, loudly abusing some of the other guests as he worked his way through the gathering. Solicitous to some, preferential treatment was blatantly transparent as they watched him hovering over a table of richly dressed Asians that looked like they were enjoying the attention, before returning to the band stand for another surreal episode of musical abuse.

"I'm telling you, this is *un destino de oportunidades"* he shouted through the mic as the audience ducked for cover.

"Opportunity for who?" Regina was shouting too, as the band abruptly broke into a Creedance Clearwater cover.

"Rollin', rollin', roooollin 'down the riii…verrr…"

"He sees himself as a visionary, but I see him as a parasite" Ruth from the village confessed to her *amigos* in disgust.

The spectacle was exploding as the wind suddenly picked up, sending a blast of sand and items from the buffet table into the infinity pool, but that didn't stop the *Two Timers.* Kicking up the tempo, the drummer went into a total frenzy, even scattering the avians that had been curiously circling all afternoon.

"I heard that they don't have clear title yet, but nobody wants to admit it?" Overheard from a table behind them, it sounded like a rumor worthy of investigation. They were all getting uncomfortable about the situation.

"When I asked him who was responsible for dredging the marina, 'cause we all know that it's not if, but when the hurricanes blast through, he joked that he didn't care, "*cause he'd be in Panama by then!*" Ruth was fed up with the phony bluster. "OMG! Can you believe it?"

Actually, the village groupies were all starting to believe... believe that it was time to skip out of the party. After a beautiful afternoon by the shore and a catered event, they knew they had already made the best of it anyway. And now that they had seen the kind of person involved in the development, they had reason to hope that the rest of the cactus just might have a chance at survival.

Joining the mass exodus, even the rattlesnakes were heading out as they abandoned their musician friends to their fate. The *Two Timers* were struggling to maintain their dignity since all the drunks wanted to sing by then, lining up to grab a turn on the microphone. Skip had slipped them each another hundred to keep playing.

"*W..ii..ii...pe .... ooo...uuu...tttt....*"

A howling surf rock drum solo on steroids followed them to the gate where everybody was watching the bus back to *Cabo* struggle to make it up the steep incline. It wasn't just the cactus in danger. Sinking deeper and deeper, the axels were disappearing into the fluffy sand, while the back of the bus careened precariously toward the edge of the steep slope of cacti. Mesmerized by the scene, they all watched until the forlorn passengers eventually filed off the bus in full surrender. Speculation about how Skip might handle the situation, his tourist and speculator guests helplessly marooned in the natural world far from *Cabo*, all led to the same scenario.

"How about another *Margarita*?" they all chorused. That seemed to be Skips answer to everything.

"'Forget about *Cactus Estates*! Too late for them now. They should rename the development *Gringo Perdido*?" Somehow Burly's sarcasm about lost *gringos* seemed appropriate under the circumstances. Since he didn't drink, he was often the designated driver. Going on to confess that as a heavy equipment operator over the years, he had probably bulldozed 400 ancient cactus. Now retired and spending half his year in Mexico, which explained his sore back, but not necessarily his cynical wit.

"Well, I think that might warrant 100,000 years in purgatory before you can be reborn as a worm!" From the backseat, Ruth felt the need to defend the lost ones, even belatedly.

"But you'll probably be forgiven because of your outstanding driving ability" Regina transparently fawned, staring out the back window over a steep drop down a rocky cliff while Burly slid closer to the edge to let three motor-cross riders blast past.

After dislodging chunks of rock to their final reckoning, Burly rose to the occasion, jamming the late model Bronco into compound low before creeping up the narrow route to freedom. Straddling the steep incline of powdery sand, the grounded bus had left barely enough room for anybody else to squeeze by. With the echo of another wild drum solo ironically marking their escape, even the stranded passengers were applauding as the *gringos* from the village disappeared into the maze of an endangered desert horizon.

Oasis

Stepping off the dusty streets of the village, the posse of *amigos* welcomed the humid shade of the oasis as a variety of mature palms towered above them to produce a patterned web of sky. The late morning was already heating up and thick vegetation along the path rustled with bird activity when a Road Runner suddenly bolted across the clearing just ahead of them, disappearing into a thicket of sprouting palms. Flowering mango trees in the oasis hummed with busy pollinators, caressing the tiny blossoms in accordance with their natural order. It was the kind of glorious day that made them all glad that they had endured the windy months that accompany a *Baja California* winter on the Tropic of Cancer.

"Is this going to be a Mexican stand-off, or what...?" Judy, visiting from the mainland, was not accustomed to the free-range practices of *BCS* and now a massive bull staunchly blocked the path ahead, impatiently stomping his hoof, anxious to lead his herd through the oasis.

"I don't think so!" Reggie instead led the *Amigos* on to a path of less resistance, detouring through an abandoned trailer park to reach the beach.

Overgrown and vandalized, it was still a place of fond memories for the *gringos* in the village who had previously wintered there, a nostalgic diversion on a mission of discovery. Managed for many years by John the *Baja Birder,* it was his web site that kept the world abreast of bird life in *Baja California.* Vistas of the Sea of Cortez sparkled through the palms as they continued on the path through the oasis, emerging to a broad swath of watery estuary thick with bird life. Scattered around the muddy circumference with cow pies, they reasoned that the murky water was brackish. An impressive pair of Wood Storks reminded them that John had spotted and documented them the day before.

After the shade of the oasis, the brilliance of the panorama was almost blinding, but after a while they were able to count half a dozen fishing boats on the horizon. Although other areas of the inland Sea of Cortez had been fished out, local fishing boats still managed to keep restaurants in the *Cabo* area supplied with fish. They were a little surprised though, to see several shrimp boats at anchor in the *Bahia,* since it was so close to the end of the season. A massive mound of beach debris on the far side of the estuary was their destination. Mystery surrounded the whole pile and like shit attracts flies, the *gringos* were on a quest to find some answers.

They had been watching the pile grow all winter, as a seemingly supernatural force had been collecting all the driftwood from the beach, even going so far as to rip out half buried trunks from under the sand. A closer inspection only brought up more questions. Bulkier than a half-dozen beached whales, the enormous mound was an enigma of forms twisted together, a natural sculpture of epic proportion.

"Driftwood is what holds the dunes together. Why would anyone want to destabilize the shoreline?" Regina posed the question they were all wondering

"I thought that turtle nesting areas were protected in *Baja?*" Visiting from the mainland, Judy had arrived with expectations.

"Why do some people seem to think they can improve the beauty of the natural world?" Nobody had an answer to any of the obvious contradictions.

"First thing we do is build a house!" Reggie declared facetiously as they deposited their belongings on the sunny side of the pile.

Then it became a giant game of pick-up-sticks as the *Amigos* entertained themselves organizing pieces of driftwood into a primitive fortress. The ancient *Pericue* tribe might not have been impressed, but finally satisfied, Reggie wedged his own personal stump into the circle and propped up a few palm fronds for shade before following his companions to the Sea for a swim before lunch.

Gentle tidal swells were mesmerizing as they swam out to the sandbar for whale-watching. It was an annual spectacle in the spring, as *California Grays* worked their way back around the Cape from their adventures in the Sea of Cortez to join *comrades* who had been wintering in the Pacific lagoons for birthing and mating, connecting for the great migration north to Alaska for summer feeding. From the sand bar they were lucky enough to see several individuals surging and blowing before there was a moment of excitement as Manta Rays were spotted circling them curiously, starkly visible in the shallow water along the edge of the sand bar.

"This is when we do the *Baja-Shuffle!*" Poncho called out, sliding his feet through the sand with each step. Rays liked to hide themselves in the sand waiting for prey and if stepped on directly, can inflict a painful sting. It was a timely reminder that the Sea was alive, including 900 fish species and 32 types of marine mammals. The naturalist Jacque Cousteau had called the Sea of Cortez *"the world's aquarium"*.

Yolanda had already laid out the picnic when the rest of the *Amigos* returned from their adventures. Chips and *guacamole*, they were getting settled in their fantastical camp for lunch when a distant vibration got their attention. A giant rumbling dust cloud was forming over the southern horizon above the *playa*.

Poncho wasn't concerned. He was way more interested in preparing the fresh oysters that he and Reggie had just collected off the rocks, prying them open with a special knife that he had made in a *Oaxaca* studio which he periodically rented for knife making. With a touch of *Tabasco* and a squeeze of lime, washed down with beer, the slippery delicacy was connecting them with the ancient tribal people that had survived over millennia on harvest from the Sea. Their crude stone tools could still be found scattered throughout the dunes alongside middens of shellfish. Abundant arrowheads and bones in the same areas indicated reliable hunting, probably game like rabbits, deer and reptiles. But in the 21st century, Yolanda the Brownie Queen was passing out magic for dessert when the persistent rumble of the dust cloud became hard to ignore. It seemed to be headed in their direction.

"Is this the beginning of another Mexican stand off?" Judy joked ironically as the vibrations from the mammoth machine began to ripple through the sand.

"Maybe we should have set up our picnic someplace else..." Yolanda trailed off, getting nervous about any confrontation with a mechanized monster.

"Don't move!" Judy commanded with sudden authority. "We don't need to feel intimidated. This is a public beach. Let's just continue our picnic." She was a child of the Sixties and willing to defy authority when necessary.

Regina decided to have another brownie.

Time slipped into a new dimension as the spectacle continued in its noisy trajectory. Radiating an apocalyptic cloud of dust in its path, it was hard to resist a sense of horror as it rattled toward them.

"I'm starting to see this as a metaphor..." Judy hypothesized, staring down the beach at the impending scenario.

A hideous reminder of the continuing New World Conquest was headed in their direction. Verging on surreal as it approached, menacing details of the pounding D9 Caterpillar had the wildlife bolting for cover. It was becoming the normal all over *Baja,* as Capitalist entrepreneurs, Canadians and Stateside Boomers searching for adventure in their retirement years were drawn to *California.* There was space. It was beautiful. It was still a land of opportunity.

"You gotta be careful what you wish for" Reggie commented ironically. "I think that some of our questions about this mystery are about to be answered."

Cracking open more drinks and settling in against their chosen stumps, they fell silent. Every steel link in the grotesque machine screeched violently as the D9 continued its relentless advance. Only Judy's stern gaze kept them all frozen as the freakish apparition of a two-story dust cloud rumbled across the beach toward them. It was mesmerizing.

When the giant calamity was about 30 meters away a figure began to emerge like a phantom from the core of the cloud. Between a baseball cap and a bandana, his sunglasses were coated with dust.

"Ignore him!" Judy ordered. "Let's just be One with the elements."

That's when a giant dirt ball rolled in and it became impossible for the *Amigos* to ignore, putting them into spastic fits of coughing until the dust settled. The rude beast was only a short distance from the picnic, its gigantic scooper facing them in a menacing way. The counterculture martyr, Rachael Corrie came to mind as they tried to compose themselves.

"Okay, he's made his point. Anybody want to play Mexican Train?"

Judy was always ready to play that popular game and all things considered, it seemed like a good idea at the time. Except for Regina who had already become "One" with the sand as the second brownie kicked in. Judy passed out the dominoes. Doing a good job of ignoring the monstrosity parked five meters away, they managed to stretch the game half an hour before the dozer operator pulled out his cell phone.

"Looks like reinforcements are on the way" Regina reported from her Sphinx position, noticing dust clouds appearing from over a rainbow horizon.

The stand-off was beginning to feel like a slap-stick episode out of a *"Monte Python"* thriller as first a caravan of pick-up trucks, followed by a caravan of SUV's with tinted windows raced toward them, dramatically speeding down the beach, churning up more clouds of dust as they arrived to line up alongside the D9. The *Amigos* recognized several members of prominent *Eijido* families as they gathered behind the big CAT for a heavy weight powwow.

Meanwhile, the *Amigos* were having their own reasoning session. Between the stand-off and the brownies, the situation was starting to feel almost comical. Even Judy was having a hard time keeping a sober face as the situation escalated.

"Okay, we've made our point" she finally admitted, standing up in surrender. A supremely symbolic moment had arrived.

"What was that point?" Poncho blurted out impulsively. "Your point or my point?"

He wasn't the only one who was curious. As each of them took a stand, there were plenty of reasons to go around. Both environmental and esthetic concerns made the oasis a Scenic Point worthy of protection, and the *Amigos* were standing in solidarity with the natural world. Watching the relentless march of development replacing precious shoreline around the *Cabo* with a landscape of cement block and glass buildings, they had seen enough evidence to be concerned.

The *Ejido* families evidentially had more than a different opinion: They had a plan for development. Symbolizing different dreams for *California,* they all realized the dilemma, but faced with a dozer operated by locals, it was the *gringos* who had to accept Conquest. It was a powerful metaphor. When a figure approached from behind the dozer, the *gringos* sent out Poncho as their representative. *California* dreaming, the wind was coming up as they began negotiations.

"Yeeeaaah! Here come the beautiful people" Reggie expounded sarcastically, kicking an old aluminum can down the path.

Vibrations from of the D-9 pushing sand into the estuary, followed the *Amigos* back through the oasis as they began their retreat.

"They're going to pave paradise and put up a parking lot ...." Regina sang from a Joni Mitchel classic, just a little off key. "What kind of beautiful is that?"

With a new sense of urgency, they had just learned the details of the calamity. Four miles of oasis beachfront, including the fresh water lagoon at the river mouth, had been sold to an unidentified consortium of investors for a luxury hotel/condominium/marina complex with a golf course. Fences going in around the oasis would make this their last adventure in Paradise. The disappointment of exile was overwhelming.

"If this oasis is an opportunity, why should it be for investors? I realize we are only guests in this country, but ...." Yolanda trailed off. As foreigners spending time in Mexico, the quandary sometimes included scenarios of disenchantment.

"Conquest has always been about resources. The beauty of this place has incredible value..." Judy pondered thoughtfully, "but it's unbelievable that the *Ejido* could have the power over this fragile ecosystem."

"Who are these people who have more money than God? You can bet they're not from around here. Too much dark money in these kind'a projects..." Reggie cynically insinuated.

"Developed in exchange for a few new trucks that will be rusting on the streets in a few years? This kind of treasure shouldn't be measured in *pesos*" Judy added with conviction. "Capitalism is out of control!"

"I just powwowed with them. It's hard to blame people for wanting to improve their lives" Poncho reminded them. "It's not just new trucks: The village *Ejido* is hoping that this project will bring jobs to the village, so that their children don't have to all move away to find work."

"Does Environmental Protection even know about this project?" Judy was still fuming. "We should find out. We should be protecting this living environment. Where do they think oxygen comes from?"

"The strength of the elements give me reason for hope." Regina was stubbornly clinging to her belief in the power of Nature. Hurricanes and tropical storms periodically pounded the East Cape, constantly changing the contours of the coastline.

"A flash flood is going to blast through the *arroyo* and sweep away any hotel or golf course in its path!" It was tempting to imagine such a possible scenario.

They had glimpsed an unwelcome future and disappointment was following them as they made their exodus from Paradise when they noticed subtle changes in the natural world. Quantum apparitions of their own surrender, the filtered shade of the oasis abruptly faded into mauve and the brooding silence was replaced by the simmering rustle of the palm canopy. Pausing to check the sky, fingers of gray were chasing away the bright blue and vultures were circling on the rising wind.

"We may not be indigenous, but we know the spirit of this place" Yolanda sighed, reaching for a colorful blossom that had fallen onto the path before her. The wind off the Sea of Cortez suddenly turned cold and a mysterious fog began crawling into the oasis delivering bright yellow butterflies that began circling her.

Creating a timely distraction, the appearance of the unexpected was enchanting. When another, then another and then a multitude of mystical beings materialized to form a pulsing yellow cloud around all of the *Amigos*, they finally noticed that the foggy foliage of the oasis was actually quivering with a spectacle of the fluttering beings.

Quantum Physics allows for particles to be in dual states at the same time and willing to suspend reason as a current of energy took wing around them, the *Amigos* accepted the presence of cosmic messengers. United in the awareness of their immanent fate, they surrendered to the enchanting migration of butterflies beginning their own exodus, joining them to flutter their way out of Paradise.

Cowgirl

'Cowgirl really didn't see it coming. How could she have? Young people were on the move at the turn of the century and the famous surf breaks along the *Baja California* Pacific coast, with it's perfect weather and abundance of organic food, had become a major year round *gringo* destination point. Cowgirl's disillusioned ex-pat parents had brought her there as a child, so that had become her reality. Attending local schools, she had learned how to take care of herself while her parents mostly made ends meet through pot growing, music and odd jobs, piecing together a life in *Baja California Sur*. A rich agricultural area to the north of *Cabo San Lucas* and close to the magical mission town of *Todos Santos*, it was an oasis village located directly on the Tropic of Cancer. Organic farming had arrived with hippy farmers from all ethnic persuasions and people mostly found ways to get along. After twenty years, the *gringo* pioneers had blended into the rural community.

Cerritos Beach was one of the infamous points attracting a lot of young surfers to it's awesome break and sweeping crescent of white sand. They were usually on the lookout for good weed, so Cowgirl was always a welcome sight, bouncing across the desert horizon in her dusty pick-up as soon as she was old enough to drive. There were no services in those early days, aside from board rentals, so making deliveries to the campers spread out along the edge of the desert became a lucrative business for her. Water, ice and beer, the young entrepreneur was soon diversified. And nobody messed with Cowgirl. Her feisty attitude more than made up for her tiny stature, her chewed up cowboy hat letting you know that you'd better think again if you thought you could take advantage of her services.

But things change. Good news spreads fast and soon the beach population swelled to include not just surfers but also swarms of the curious. The surf shack expanded to include horse, kayak and quad rentals. The old, decayed RV Park overlooking the beach was sold to developers and fences started to go up. A surf colony sprouted luxury *palapas* while an old surfer with mis-guided imagination built a castle on the bluff. After a while, a beach club was constructed right on the sand, serving drinks and food to the hordes of tourists hungering to be part of the scene. Sunday afternoons were especially lucrative, with live music creating the kind of ambience that makes you want to drink or score before signing up for a surf lesson or relaxing under a beach umbrella for a massage.

With rising demand, business was good for Cowgirl, but she wanted it to be better. By then she was a single mother, and the pressure was on to provide for her son when a new boyfriend from *Sinaloa* helped her to expand her merchandising into hard drugs. Before long she was also developing a market among the locals. Naively, she was creating a monster.

Rumor was that a *Cartel* was involved. Wanting to invest their heaps of illicit dollars, they were setting up family members in legitimate businesses wherever they saw opportunity. *La Paz*, on the Sea of Cortez had already been invaded and a battle was raging between two rival gangs and the *Policia* for territory and booty. Intimidating the authorities through torture, murder and even be-headings, the rampage began spilling over into nearby smaller communities, especially those that included tourist destinations.

Cowgirl was living large when she got the news.

"You're working for us now."

It had been an awesome day at *Cerritos*, with *Daline* crooning from the little stage out front of the Surf Club, her up-beat jazzy style creating a mellow beach scene for the mixture of locals and tourists that were lucky enough to be there. Behind her, a nice north swell was bringing in impressive waves for the surfers. Ravishing in white, with roses in her hair, *Daline* looked like she had just stepped out of a cloud as she floated around the stage.

"Don't Worry, Be Happy...."

Big Dumb Bob was right up front encouraging the ladies to get up and dance. Even the whales were hanging in closer to the beach, spy-hopping to catch every beat while the *loco* packs of loose dogs were getting along fine for a change. Cowgirl was heading home early when she was cornered in the parking lot.

"Fuck you!" she shouted, loud enough to draw attention. "I've been working this beach since I was sixteen. Who are you? You're not even from around here"

Evidently the three bad asses weren't satisfied, moving in on the defiant girl to make themselves absolutely clear, grabbing her arm tightly for extra effect. Whatever they said, Cowgirl didn't like it.

"Get over it!" she unloaded on them. "I'm the *choyerra* here - I'm the local, so get used to it." Pulling herself free, they didn't follow her and the trail of her dust soon settled into the darkening afternoon horizon of the *Lagunas de las Sierras*.

"But you don't understand, I've been threatened! We've all been threatened and I'm not going to take it from those *pinche cabrones* - dumb goat suckers! We need protection and I'm going to the *Policia.*" It hadn't taken Cowgirl long to make a plan, but her family wasn't convinced.

"Leaping lizards Cowgirl, it sounds like the *Cartel* is implicated here and I'm afraid that our local police might be too intimidated by organized crime to protect us. It's *plata o plomo*, silver or lead, and I heard that most of the force hasn't even been paid in months. It comes down to survival for them and their families." Cowgirl's father was searching for a realistic alternative, but all he could come up with was surrender.

"No! We are not going to be driven out of business by some dumb J*efes* that up and decide that they can intimidate us or our village. Our community isn't up for grabs and we need to stand together. I know every officer on the force. Hey, I sell weed to some of them! Just who do you think they're going to stand with? This is their territory too." For Cowgirl, it was an obvious choice.

Evidently the *Policia* had already heard about "The Flamingo". As soon as Cowgirl mentioned his name and said that she wanted to testify, the *Federales* were notified. The day after that, the military arrived, looking tough with their black face masks, making a big scene for a while with their camouflage vehicles heavily loaded with armed soldiers ready for action.

Writing reports of the incident and preparing a statement for her to sign almost seemed patriotic to Cowgirl who was temporarily feeling invincible. Then she learned that *La Paz* had experienced over fifty murders in the last year and she was officially warned to keep a low profile for a while. Coupled with last months shoot-out at the local PEMEX station, it looked like their little seaside village was becoming another flash point in the notorious *War on Drugs* and little Cowgirl had become part of the story.

The gardener saw them coming first, sleazily crawling down the steep dirt road behind the house in a white pickup with darkened windows. They shot him as he was trying to make an escape over a barbed wire fence, leaving him to dangle as they turned their attention toward the house and their intended victim. As soon as she heard the shots Cowgirl ran upstairs with her little son and shoved him under the bed as they opened fire on the house with automatic weapons. The assassins had seen her brief glance from a downstairs window, so that became their target and that was probably what saved them. After a rain of bullets, they sped off in a cloud of dust, leaving the dead gardener and echoes of terror to ricochet through the neighborhood and beyond.

Before Cowgirl even had time to assess the damage, a whole squadron of military commandos descended on them in full combat mode, surrounding the neighborhood with all their latest U.S. military surplus vehicles, pumped up and ready for action while neighbors helplessly looked on from behind bolted doorways.

"You set me up!" she unloaded on the *Comindante* defiantly. "How could you be here so fast unless you knew what was coming down?"

Of course Cowgirl was crazed, but she was starting to realize what her father had been talking about: Militarization of law enforcement in Mexico was creating increasingly warlike interdiction. With statistics like 80,000 deaths and 200,000 displacements since 2006, law enforcement and the judicial institutions appeared to often be corrupt and inefficient. For the sake of funding from the *U.S.A. War on Drugs,* violent crime by the security forces themselves was being ignored.

Cowgirl and her family were everyone's target now.

❦

"And you still want to kick-butt?" Cowgirl's neighbor was incredulous. "What about the threat to your family and neighbors?"

The dust had barely settled after the drive-by and while the family was inside emotionally evaluating their options, outside there was an outpouring of grief. An impromptu shrine was materializing on the ragged fence where Cowgirl's gardener had so shortly before been pruning. Flowers, mementos and pictures were appearing in a desperate plea for mercy, flowing into the street where the blood of an innocent, still drying in the dust, had so recently been spilled.

"I'm not going to run away" Cowgirl promised with righteous conviction, stooping to pick up a bullet shell that the swarm of soldiers had overlooked.

"But there is no doubt that you all have to go into hiding for a while. We don't know who to trust anymore. I've got space at my house and they'll never expect you to be so close by." Their neighbor was trying to maintain calm, but everyone was talking at once.

"We could go to the mountains and camp out for a while." This suggestion from Grandpa had Little Cowboy racing upstairs to pack his toys, but Grandma had ideas of her own.

"Little Cowboy can't go to school here, he might get kidnapped! Let's go to *La Paz* and just blend in."

"Get a few things together and I'll sneak you up to my place tonight. Otherwise, you'll never get any sleep here. It's not safe for you or your family, and you can all stay with me until you figure out a plan." Bribing her friends with chocolate, Kitty wasn't taking no for an answer.

For two weeks the sun still came up in the morning to the tweets of migrating birds greeting another beautiful day in paradise. Overlooking the bountiful oasis, the fugitives watched the farmers laying out neat rows of young chili peppers and every afternoon the cumulous skies of mid-winter created another spectacular sunset. But Cowgirl was getting impatient, not even trying to keep her whereabout secret anymore. Pacing around the compound in broad daylight, it wasn't long before the neighbors began to get nervous and when fear creeps in, things get weird. The day came when a confrontation was inevitable: For the safety of the community, the fugitives had to go.

Cowgirl had been planning their getaway. Her parents would take their grandson into hiding in the mountains, while Cowgirl would be connecting with the boyfriend from *Sinaloa* to consider their options.

"They've offered me silver and now they've given me lead! First thing I'm doing is getting a gun of my own, so I can protect myself."

"Please don't escalate your predicament" Kitty pleaded urgently. She was willing to shelter her friends, but still, there was an obvious question that needed to be asked. "Why not return to the States for awhile?"

"We have everything invested in our lives here." The family stood together, united in their belief that there was no standing down now. Chocolate wasn't going to work anymore. They had all stopped listening.

Ports of Illusion

The Source Family, The Farm, the Isaiah Truthteller Family, Back to the Earth, were all counter culture movements of the 1960's that tried to resurrect the old models of rural communal living during a period of rampant corporate expansionism. Families and tribes were springing up all over the country, fed by massive disillusionment with Capitalist culture that was trying to turn everything into a commodity.

"Everybody wanted to be a part of a movement that was challenging the status quo." Rummaging through her bag, Constanza finally scored, pulling out a ragged photo to share with her *amigos*. Taken in San Francisco in 1970, it was a glimpse at a cultural turning point: An epic caravan of painted hippie buses queuing up in San Francisco's Golden Gate Park, for a massive migration back to sustainability.

"I think these are the busses led by counter culture icons Steven and Ina Mae Gaskin" she pointed out. "That caravan was on it's way to establishing The Farm in Tennessee." Her amigos fumbled through their bags for spectacles, hoping for a clearer picture of the historical event.

"At the same time Israel Love was taking his flock north to Oregon. When you joined the family you were expected to share everything you owned in order to surrender to the needs of the larger family. Changing our names was only a part of it" Constanza dreamily reminisced. "Love, Brotherhood, Creativity, Patience, Charity and Wisdom became the deacons that would lead the way to the promised land."

Pausing to enjoy their own version of the promised land, the four *Amigos* became fixated on a pair of graceful white egrets in flight across the tantalizing, azure lagoon, their reflections disappearing into the shelter of mangroves. First claimed for Spain by Cortez in 1535, they were close to the charming old world city of *La Paz,* the capital of *Baja California Sur,* past the small craft harbor and luxury hotels scattered along the coast, past the ferry terminal onto the *Pichilingue Peninsula,* where the desert meets the Sea and the white sandy shores of *Balandra* Bay welcome an appreciative locals and visitors to enjoy it's panoramic vistas. The natural elements include dozens of islands, 900 varieties of fishes, 5000 micro-invertebrates, as well as marine mammals and the ever-popular Whale Sharks that visitors loved to swim with.

It was a postcard perfect morning and the *Amigos* could hardly believe that they had the beach to themselves. They had walked around a Scenic Point to a place so private that it was easy to be seduced by the seclusion, so they got naked, a cultural taboo in Mexico's very conservative culture. Carnival's Fat Tuesday celebrations had mandated a beach day for them, but evidently the rest of the partiers were still sleeping it off after too much of everything; an exotic parade of floats and festively costumed revelers; loudly competing vendors selling merchandise that you didn't know that you wanted; multiple venues presenting Mexico's top musical performers and a glittering arcade to trip out in. The *Amigos* now knew why Carnival week in La Paz has a reputation for meltdowns. They were moving slow as Tahoe passed around a joint.

"Brotherhood usually organized the Meltdowns for the Family..." Constanza made circles in the sand while she thought about her story.

"Those were the musical episodes that brought the Families together for community building. Often his sister Virtue and I would help out."

Constanza was now living half the year in *Baja*, a Snowbird, part of a growing tribe of aging baby-boomers spending their winters south of the border. Adjusting her bosom onto the warm sand, Constanza squirmed a little while relating some details of her time spent with the Love Family.

"We'd go as a Family to the Rainbow gatherings, which were so empowering, making us all realize our shared goals and how connected all people are, but when we got home, the experience would fade..." she quietly confessed. "Not unlike other communal family groups splintering off from fading fantasies of the 60's, in retrospective, things had not always been what they had seemed. After years of surrender, people began to ask questions. Contrary to what he preached, Israel didn't like being confronted with uncomfortable questions and eventually some family members started to scatter. Now we all stay connected through the WorldWideWeb. Currently we are going to the *Laundromat*, an

Internet sounding board for dredging up old feelings in order to clear the air. Just what had happened during that episode and how we're feeling about it now? As the *Age of Aquarius* led us all in new and often separate directions, you can imagine that some issues have given us a lot to talk about" she finished. Standing to discover sand on her privates, she was ready to change the subject.

"Hey, let's go swimming!"

Ignoring Tahoe's reminder to "Baja Shuffle!" to scatter any stingrays, Regina plunged after Constanza into the crystal water of the lagoon. It was like emersion with a precious gem, rinsing off sand and any lingering doubt that it might all be an illusion.

Reality worked it's magic as the time passed and eventually the *Amigos* were dreaming of cold drinks with *comidas*. When they got back to the parking lot, Tahoe lit up another joint. Traveling the short distance along Hwy. 11 to *Tecolote*, the women were in the back seat struggling to get their clothes back on over damp bodies, when they drove right into a military checkpoint.

"*Santa Maria,* open the windows!" Reggie demanded, while the passengers in the back seat panicked.

"Reggie, we're still half naked!"

But it was too late. Their vehicle was already surrounded by teenagers with automatic weapons. Flying brassieres and a turmoil of clothing had greeted their demands to get out of the vehicle, but the two women weren't yet ready for the untimely inspection.

"*Me espossa no tiene pantelones!*" - "My wife has no pants on!" Reggie raggedly explained to the dazed young corporal in charge, stalling for time. "*Un momento, por favor.*"

Probably bored, the young soldiers immediately rushed the vehicle, hopefully peaking into the half-opened windows for a little cheap entertainment, while Tahoe and Reggie carefully stepped out onto the sandy roadway. The women were blushing with embarrassment when they finally emerged for their own inspection.

The young Corporal seemed embarrassed too, and was easily satisfied that there were no hidden guns or ammunition in the car. Evidently, they were too distracted to even be concerned about the lingering scent of *marijuana*, because the suspects were soon waved on.

"What would they do with the four of us in jail anyway?" Reggie joked.

"Considering that there is cartel violence all over Mexico, they are probably just trying to keep us safe." Regina had put on her rose colored glasses.

"I heard that the cartels are moving away from the border towns now, into interior cities" Reggie tossed into the mix, " and I've noticed more graffiti around La Paz. Maybe it's just an illusion."

"Locals here do call *La Paz* the *Port of Illusion*. It becomes too easy to lose ourselves in the beauty of this place, but we have to remember that we are guests here in Mexico." Tahoe was usually the final authority on the subtle nuance of Mexican culture. "Always remember to shuffle your feet!"

"I can't wait" Constanza teased, pushing her foot around the seat to give Tahoe a playful stroke.

"I actually thought we would have to bribe our way out of that one" Tahoe confessed, checking the contents of his wallet. "I guess the women were enough of a distraction, Reggie. We'll have to remember that diversion in the future!" Now that the encounter was past, he wanted to get back to playful illusion, but his tactless suggestion kept the women riled up all the way to *Tecolote*.

Surrounded by cactus studded mountains and dramatic rock formations, *Tecolote* was a favorite camping spot for eco-tourists wanting to explore the unique environment of the *Pichilingue Peninsula*. Several make-shift buildings set up along the beach offered meals for those not wanting to rough it and one establishment was actually a ship-a-shore propped up in the sand.

Settling into a surf-side table at the Restaurante ORION, with "*Margaritas*" on the way, the recent episode began to fade, leaving the *Amigos* with only a vague sense of violation. The tide was turning and little rivulets were starting to reach their table while they watched fishing boats returning from *Isla Espiritu Santo*, pulling in further down the beach with their catch. Pearling may have attracted early fortune seekers, but fishing was a more recent staple.

"*Si, tenemous pescado* - We have fish" the waiter replied as they asked about the menu. "It's becoming a challenge though. A decade ago, fisherman could catch their limit, and now they return with just a few fish."

"Hey, you speak good English." Regina was appreciative.

"*Gracias*. I worked for many years in the States, but there is more opportunity here now, so I returned to be with my family."

"We were almost fished out in the Monterey Bay of Central California" Reggie explained to their host, "but a five year moratorium brought back the fish and now fishing is strictly regulated."

"International pirates are taking our fish. They come in with nets and longlines when our Navy is in port. Lately, our local *pescadores* are being sabotaged. Their boats have been stolen and later found adrift with the motors chain sawed out." It was a familiar story of yet another natural resource being pushed to the edge.

After some sober discussion about sport fishermen exceeding the limits of the past and bragging about it, they decided it was time for another *Margarita* and a little attitude adjustment. With the tide lapping at their ankles, even faced with the dilemma of extinction, the *Amigos* still managed to enjoy their crispy fried fish feast along the edge of the Sea of Cortez.

La Perla was an open air restaurant overlooking the crescent of the Bahia, a comfortable refuge from the excesses of the big city, especially after Carnival. What had for nights been a crazy kaleidoscope of revelry and celebration, with troops of wildly costumed dancers and full watt entertainment, was finally a scene of peace again. Skaters and bikers zig-zagged along the sidewalk between public works of art, families and couples were enjoying an evening stroll along the popular sidewalk. The iconic *Arch of Illusion* framed the sunset, as the lights along the *Malecon* turned on under a deep crimson sky.

"Ahhhh... , flan at La Perla! It's a tradition!" Regina had been saving room for dessert. "Smooth and creamy, that's how I like it!"

"Why is flan a tradition?" Posed ready with a spoonful of the creamy custard that Mexican cuisine has made famous, Constanza was curious about such an expansive claim.

Reggie jumped in to tell the story. "We had been camping out at *Tecolote* with Captain and Yolanda. We were playing music around the campfire, when it got crazy windy, turning into a waltz of the Four Winds! We were getting sand blasted until we made an escape into our tents for the night."

"Plus we had to make room for the dogs!" Regina reminded him.

Reggie went on to describe the howling of the wind and the flapping of the tent sides that had kept them awake all night in a state of desperation.

"After spending the night on our hands and knees, by first light we were so exhausted that the only thing we could think about was surrender. The stuff that didn't get blown away during the night, got blown away while we were packing up!"

"We were pathetic! As soon as we could get to *La Paz* we came here for some coffee and comfort food." Pausing for another bite, Regina got dreamy at that point in the story. Savoring the creamy essence, accompanied by appropriate sound effects, she was very convincing. "I still believe that La Perla has the best flan in the universe! Mmmmm…"

"Now we have another *Tecolote* story! I'm still laughing about our recent interrogation." Constanza got them all giggling self-consciously as they reviewed the untimely roadblock experience and soon they were all howling with laughter. "Of course, laughing didn't quite seem like an option at the time!"

Meanwhile, a frightening episode was unfolding along the *Malecon*. A first impression was that it might have been a movie shoot. Erratically disregarding the mellow vibe of a Mexican tourist destination, a young cowgirl in sexy shorts and stiletto cowboy boots was running along the street with a drawn pistol. Behind her a white pickup with tinted windows was zig-zagging through traffic, scattering pedestrians along the sidewalk with semi-automatics aimed right at the cowgirl. Noticing a *Policia* roadblock forming on the next block, it looked like it might be Cowgirl's best chance.

When the shooting started, they still weren't actually sure it was the real thing, until a grenade landed right in Regina's flan, scattering the sticky delicacy all over the four of them. Abruptly slipping from illusion to reality, they stared at the sticky time bomb for only a second before joining the rest of the diners madly evacuating the premises. A *chubasco,* a storm of epic dimension, they all bolted past the Jazz Trio, skipping the music to tumble over the railing onto the *Plaza Constitution* where the sidewalk cafes were just coming to life. They never actually heard an explosion, but echoes from the firestorm erupting back on the *Malecon* followed them for blocks while they raced for safety.

Startled tourists and curious shopkeepers just opening after *siesta*, didn't get any explanation as they fled past the old stone Watchtower and along the *Boulevard 16th of September,* their route including a maze of infrastructure projects. Weaving through scaffolding, Regina struggling to keep up with her posse, Reggie half dragging her through the obstacles of a city tortured by detours. Dodging between stalled traffic, banging into low hanging air conditioners and jumping over unmarked holes in the sidewalk and random piles of construction materials. Layers of history released from loose cobblestones; in a different time they might have been escaping from pirates. Finally careening into the relative safety of a counter culture beacon of revolutionary activism, they collapsed together around a table in the lush interior patio of the *Yeneka Arte Hotel.*

"Who was that cowgirl? Reggie demanded pointlessly. "Can just anybody get a pistol now?"

"I hope this doesn't become another crazy tradition" Constanza managed to joke sarcastically. "I'd rather be suspended in the illusions of the 60's counterculture." Her wild silver hair was electrified.

"It's hard to imagine that we'll be laughing about this episode in the future" panted Tahoe cryptically, hoping that he wasn't having a heart attack.

The *Amigos* were all talking at once, reporting the bizarre story to the inquisitive German writer that called the strange hotel home. He had lived there three years, writing a book that was by then he claimed to be 1,847 pages long. His bushy gray beard was quivering slightly as he responded solemnly to reports of the latest crazy chapter.

"This place has always been a *Port of Illusion*" he expounded, "all of us attracted here by the natural beauty. Early peoples were invaded by Conquistadors, then conquered by disease. Missionaries had to flee from rebellious Guayacura, and now Cartels and Oligarchs want control. Through Invasion, Conquest, tourists and Pirates, *La Paz* is continually forced into becoming a modern version of itself. History has not alway been peaceful, but because of its beauty, the illusion has somehow endured."

Surrounded by decades of historical clutter and weird decor, rusty relics, faded portraits of Freida Kahalo and infamous Mexican revolutionaries staring out at them from a mosaic of brightly painted walls over an alter created from the grill of an old Pontiac, the moldy stuffed monkey perched behind the wheel of the antique panel truck parked there in the tropical courtyard, didn't seem quite so bizarre anymore.

Lords of the Wind

"Mama, you told me there weren't going to be any problems!"

On their way to the annual *Lord of the Winds Kiteboarding Showdown* on the East Cape, the sudden appearance of a military checkpoint a short distance ahead hadn't been in the plans.

"I guess I'm going to have to take responsibility for that information" Reggie cut in, trying to avoid an untimely marital dispute in the front seat. "I told you there've been a few loco incidents in *Baja* recently, but this area has stayed mostly *tranquillo. Lo siento, amigos*, my apologies."

"Let's just turn around and go back to the *casa,* Papa." Although their son had recently moved on to college, the couple were still clinging to familial endearments.

"NO!" Her spouse was adamant. "We can't draw that kind of attention right now. Never show fear in these kinds of situations!" A martial arts teacher, Papa was already taking a defensive posture as their vehicle was waved into the detour.

"No drogas!" No drugs Reggie volunteered from the back seat window before the dust had even settled. "We don't have any guns. *No hay pistolas*" he added, using his best Spanish accent in an effort to neutralize the situation.

The *Comandante* stared at them without expression, indicating with his semi-automatic that they should get out of their car. Surrounded by heavily armed soldiers with face coverings, the gringos stood their ground while the inspection proceeded.

"If they were looking for drugs, they'd have knocked the tires. They're checking for guns" Reggie surmised as they pulled away from the check point. Then as they proceeded, the *gringos* wondered if the soldiers had noticed the suspicious truck kicking up dust on the far crest of the road as he spun his wheels in an abrupt detour.

"Looks like that *hombre* doesn't want to be inspected" they all agreed as the mysterious truck disappeared over the next rise.

A sense of adventure was returning when a couple of Roadrunners bolted across the *camino* in front of them. After that, skirting a herd of wild donkeys grazing alongside the road was romantic for the visitors. A couple of babies at their mother's side were heart melting.

"I guess I was overreacting, Papa. I feel better now. The simplicity of the open range is renewing my hope for the world." We each create our own reality and Mama usually tried to keep things on the sunny side.

Still Dreaming California

"Right" Reggie added cryptically, "until you hit a black cow at two minutes to midnight! We're all gonna die!"

But he soon regretted his impulsive remarks as they reached the next curve to discover another road block ahead. This time a squadron of military vehicles surrounding a late model sedan with doors ominously agape and two men laying face down in the dust with their arms bungeed behind them. The *gringos* had just barely made it to a full stop when a camouflaged military truck dramatically swerved in front of them to disgorge another squadron of soldiers to join their *comrades*, swarming onto the surrounding desert, on the hunt for the ones that got away.

"Papa...." But Papa wasn't going for it.

"I agree with Reggie. This is about guns. They're not looking for us Mama, so let's just stay cool." Papa was probably hoping that no one would notice the sweat erupting from his own neck.

"Look at that!" Reggie exploded as Extremo Nemo came in on the bank, making a monster landing right in front of the judges with Fritz scoring a big one right behind him. Wiping the splash from her face, Regina wasn't quite as enthusiastic.

"Do we have to be sitting so close!" The tide was coming in, running up the bank now close to their feet, but her words were lost in the wind. The spectators were hunkering down along the shoreline with hoodies laced tight as the racers battled the torment of the Sea.

Sponsored by the *Rotary Club of Los Barriles* and *Baja Sports* as a fundraiser for the community, the SHOWDOWN is the premiere kiting event in Mexico, determining who will be the reigning North American Kite Champion. In addition to creating wind sport royalty, the festival also provides valuable exposure for wind sport companies and their rapidly evolving sports gear.

Booths set up on the beach behind the grandstand were displaying the latest gear along with t-shirts, food and *cerveza*. Affiliated festivities and spin off activities guarantee that a good time would be had by all. The event was attracting international attention, fast becoming a destination point for the developing wind surfing and kiteboarding sports world.

"**Hey! Go Monster!**" screamed Grom Gormley the announcer from his vantage point on the scaffolding behind them, while scantily clothed *Corona Girls* on the top tier lustily cheered on the contestants. "**Quite a ride! Ultraaaah!**"

Waving to the crowd, #35 sped by high on his foil. Airborne, he easily cleared the buoy marking the bottom of the course.

Kite-Boarders harness the power of the wind with controllable kites that pull the rider across the water on a board with the ability to launch the rider into the air when desired. Kite technology was becoming very specialized with equipment designs for every event, leading to greater safety along with faster rides.

"**Five, four, three, two, one**" and a rude blast from a bullhorn let the competitors and everyone else know that the heat was over, while the crowd erupted in applause for D.J. Guacamole dancing his way back up the beach with the next heat crisscrossing into position behind him.

A group gasp came up as Synbad floated by the beach resting on her hydrofoil three feet above the surface, skimming through the surf line like a dragonfly. One of *Los Barriles'* own, she was kiting professionally, showing off her big air skills for the locals there cheering her on. The north wind blows down the Sea of Cortez from mid-November through mid-March producing sustained winds and rolling swells that have attracted an enthusiastic posse of seasonal kiters who call the East Cape their home away from home. Reggie let out a piercing whistle as Synbad banked into a wave and went airborne.

"Hey Real Time, one minute 'til the start of the next event!" Another blast from the bullhorn left no mystery about that.

"**Fiona has the green kite out front**" Grom explained, "**while Chelsea with the black kite is coming in fast. Good air! She's killin 'it!**" His excitement howled out into the wind. Big Air is one of the most physically challenging events of the competition with the explosive lifting power of the kites pulling riders as much as 40 feet into the air.

"Oooohhh..." then "Ahhhh..." The crowd was disappointed as Chelsea flopped the landing, losing her board as the kite dragged her into the surf.

"**Thirty seconds left in the heat! Two of these girls will be advancing to the finals... and the rest will just be watching.**" Even though she didn't get much airtime, Fiona had made the most of it, displaying great form with a neat back loop through the surf break and a nice landing right in front of the judges.

Freestyle was the next event and the crew from *ProWindsurfing Ventana* were really taking it up a notch with an array of new and old school tricks from back loops to sliding goiters, spocks and handle-passes.

"**Hey Master of Disaster, taking a little crash. And here comes Harry! Everything's perfect in his world**" as he demonstrated his skill with a full airborne rotation and a board-off wave to the judges.

"**Looks like good manners**" Grom encouraged as Harry made a perfect landing right in front of the crowd on the beach.

Turning up the sound system for a break and sign-ups for the next event, the relentless pulse of Daft Punk with Stevie Wonder, blasted out onto the Sea of Cortez; *"Weeee've gone too faaar...*

to not knoow... where we arrrre... So let's reeach for the stars... We're up all night to get lucky..."

The crowd was all feeling lucky. A group that Reggie played music with, *Flat Dog,* a popular local R&R band had kicked off the SHOWDOWN at *Smokey's* mid-week, followed by the Reggae Dance Party at *Spa Buena Vista* on Friday nite. A Sandcastle Competition out in front of *Palmas de Cortez* was an ongoing activity.

"Hey *vato*! I haven't had this much fun since the hogs stampeded my sister." It was Jerry from New Mexico, a drummer who had been trying to get a jam session going with Reggie and Kelly, a singer/guitarist from Montreal. "We're looking for a bass player."

Reggie was always up for new musical escapades, so he and Jerry went off to collect some refreshments while they talked about it. Mama and Papa, their visitors from Northern California went down the beach to check out the Sandcastles. Regina was still riveted to the wild scene of criss-crossing kites when Grom decided to throw out some souvenirs and an event T-shirt landed right in her lap.

"Hey nothing but style!" he shouted out from the top of the scaffolding as a friendly shuffle broke out on the beach for airborne event hats, spinning around like frisbees in the wind.
Regina lay back into the sand and floated off on a cloud that reminded her of a flying turtle, recalling a different scene, half a generation ago when hordes of fishing boats would have been anchored all along the shore of the Bahia, ready to pounce on any sign of big fish. But that was long ago and even the fish killers were still arguing about what had caused the collapse.

Oh, "it was illegal fishing by foreigners" or "it was the long liners that took all the fish" or "the currents have changed", seldom wanting to face their own likely complicity in the mysteri-

Still Dreaming California

ous development. Big game fishing of a previous generation was being replaced now by a new generation of fanatics in search of wind and swell, young people that were harnessing the wind for their thrills.

"Maybe there will be a chance for the fish now" Regina mused, shifting her gaze to the north where beached kites colorfully littered the sand toward *Buenas Aires a*nd the desert landscape leading to *Pescadero.*

Peppered now by *Gringo-landia,* Regina could remember looking at the lots in that development when the hillside below the cliffs was first being marked out with orange flags. It seemed curious at the time, but in hindsight, "we should have been freaking out!"

The pristine hillside that she remembered had been mortally wounded during the following episode in *Baja* history: the Real Estate Bubble. Good economic times in the States had led to rampant real estate speculation, even in Mexico. Boomers had discovered spectacular *Baja California* after the Trans-Peninsula Highway had upgraded the historical *El Camino Real* and when they were finally doing well financially, they wanted a slice of paradise. Surrounded by the Santa Fe style architecture that had now come to be called *Mexico-Lite,* ex-pats were living their dream. Of course after the Bubble burst, many dreams had been abandoned, but not before the land had endured the trauma of rampant development that had left ugly scars.

"Thirty seconds 'til the start of Border-Cross." Grom was emphatic as he announced that this was the most exciting race on the planet to watch.

" **For entertainment value, each heat starts on the beach with riders standing on a post, chugging a beverage before running to the water and completing two laps around a floating obstacle course. There are no other rules!"**

The drum track was synchronized with Reggie's return as he settled into the sand next to his wife, just in time for the start of the first heat.

"I have some disturbing news, my darling."

He had to get close to be heard, reminding her of the recent arrival of a rumbling caravan of quads, blowing up the dust along the beach road behind the festival. Regina had fun riding Quads herself, but they could be dangerous. Quad traffic on the beach was becoming a concern as more and more crazy road warrior vehicles were tearing up the *Baja* dunes. She thought maybe someone had been hurt, but she hadn't expected to hear that a dead man had been discovered hanging from the *Buenas Aires* bridge.

"The locals say it was a drug deal gone bad for that *hombre*."

"Pura Vida will be playing for the Award Ceremony tonight at Parque de la Laguna." Grom's announcement rolled out over the Sea of Cortez. **"Be there when we award the big bucks to the event winners. Who will be the next Lord or Lady of the Wind?"**

That question was left blowing in the wind, along with the corpse, as Reggie and Regina came to the same realization: When there's a showdown, there are also going to be losers.

The event had come to its relentless finale. The news about the hanging hadn't made it onto the sound system, but looking around at the spectators, they could see that the frightening news was spreading through the crowd.

"Who was the Lord of the Wind?" Mama and Papa were back from the land of Sand Castles. Reggie and Regina had promised them Disneyland and now that allusion had been blown away.

"Hello from the other side.... Don't underestimate the things that I will do... You reap just what you soo-oo-oo-

ow..." Adelle's lyrics blasting out to sea, seemed somehow prophetic as the event abruptly ended.

"Rolling in the dee-ee-ep.... We could have had it aaaaa-AA-AA-ALL!"

Under a crimson stratus cloudscape, the wind was blasting the last spectators on the beach into retreat, quads creating a mini dust storm as they fanned out in every direction.

Joining the stampede, the *amigos* soberly surrendered with the tattered remains of their own illusions. The artificial light radiating from the growing development across the Bahia was a challenge to the brooding glow of a full moon emerging from the hazy horizon.

Path of Miracles

Dawn had begun at *San Ignacio,* with the *Camino Real* and the approaching day pulling Reggie and Regina west into a dense fog flooding in from *Ojo de Libre* and extending across *Baja California's* Central Desert. The area around *Vizcaino* marked a major shift in the seasons, with flowers blooming between Yucca trees and Century plants exuberantly announcing Spring. Home to as many as 80 varieties of cacti, plants that can survive on very little precipitation, their spongy trunks absorb water from Pacific fog. The world's largest cactus, the *Cordon,* grows up to 60 feet tall. Towering *Cirio* trees were similar to giant upside-down carrots. *Elephante* trees twisting off of inflated trunks that really do look like elephant anatomy. Together they cast long shadows through the early morning rainbow mist, like fingers of the ancestors guiding them toward *Guerero Negro* and memories of past whale watching expeditions.

The landscape became more barren as the travelers climbed the mountain to *Jesus y Maria* where a Pemex gas station, two locations for spare parts, and the Tamale Lady stood out bravely on it's stark plateau. Stopping for gas and a quick snack of tamales before continuing their homeward trek, this was a familiar outpost, memorable for past hospitality.

"*Como estas, mis Amigos?*"

Greeting them with smiles and hugs, the Tamale Lady's happy disposition overshadowed the obvious devastation of recent Pacific storms. In the tradition of the Mission Fathers, she had been feeding weary travelers for many years on a stretch of the *Camino Real* between *El Rosario* and *Guererro Negro* where services were sparse to non-existent. Her homemade *tamales* may have been famous out of proportion to their humble origin, but they had metaphorically become part of the Sacred Expedition. Before the big storm, her shabby van had always parked in front of the Pemex station under the only big shade tree in *Jesus y Maria,* but this year the tree was gone.

"*Santa Maria! Nuestra supervivencia fue un milagro!:* Our survival was a miracle!" She was animated as she described the force of the elements that had almost blown her community off of their remote plateau.

"*Gracias a Dios!*"

The Tamale Lady was rebuilding, but instead of the inviting shade of her former location, God and her husband had replaced it with a crude structure of plywood and corrugated metal that seemed fragile against the vast expanse surrounding it.

"*Si! Tengo tamales.*" As she hospitably faded into the shadows to lift the lid of an immense steaming pot, Reggie and Regina slipped into her tiny dining room. Large enough for only one plastic table and a couple of chairs, the dogs would have to wait outside. Taking up the space of another possible table, an alter to the *Virgin de Guadalupe* blazed with candles. Miraculously, the Tamale Lady had managed to remain faithful through her recent misfortunes.

Noticing that the PEMEX station at the intersection to L.A. Bay still looked abandoned, the travelers were glad that they had filled up in *Jesus y Maria*. A couple of dusty pick-ups parked at the corner were loaded with containers of gas in case of an emergency. Remembering past adventures in windy L.A. Bay, they waved their appreciation before continuing on the seriously rutted stretch of road leading towards *Catavina*.

A recent rain was evident, with cumulous layers scattering across an azure sky. The Mission Fathers had sprinkled mustard seeds to mark the path as they traveled up and down *California* and. Regina thanked them as she went crazy with her camera, trying to capture the colorful route along the *Camino* as they traveled toward the border.

The area surrounding *Catavina* was shocking in its beauty, with panoramic vistas of crazy, boulder stacked mountains dotted with colorful patches of flowers. Millions of years old, Baja's granite core had been exposed by erosion, creating a strange landscape of smooth rounded rocks and massive piles of weathered boulders strewn across the desert like a bubble machine pumping at full speed.

An isolated military checkpoint was a reminder that this was still a protected area. It's tidy roadside encampment included a sports field and Regina could see the diversity among the soldiers. Coming from all parts of Mexico, recruits were forming national camaraderie. Hundreds of kilometers from civilization, travelers could only hope that the teenagers in charge were also enjoying the view.

A prehistoric Blue Palm oasis crowding in on the roadway, signals the arrival to *Catavina*. This was the point where the Trans-peninsula Highway had met during construction in 1973. Travelers along this sparsely populated part of the *Camino Real* were most likely to stop at the *La Pinta* hotel, where a small gas pump out front provided an illusion of civilization. Pulling over across the street from that illusion, Reggie and Regina were glad that the restaurant there was still unpretentious.

"It might not rain here very often, but you'd think that they would want to cover up those holes in the roof anyway" Regina muttered privately as she and her partner let the dogs out for a stretch. There were still a few patches of snow in the shady area behind the outhouse. The mountainous area around Catavina receives only a couple of inches of rain or snow, a year, but the *palapa* roof of the family operated enterprise was perennially full of gaping holes. Ponies tied to the hitching post out front, alongside several beat up trucks and a stray donkey, made it obvious that the ramshackle building was nonetheless at the heart of the mountain community.

"No big deal. The atmosphere here is always friendly and the food is authentic." Reggie was ready for another break.

There was always a big, blackened kettle on the pot belly stove that was keeping the heat on for locals and weary travelers seeking reprieve from the cold. A happy hum was coming from the kitchen as they settled down at a table pushed up against an entertaining photo wall. Crazy customized All-terrain Trucks and Sport Utility Vehicles, motorcycles and fabricated buggies, reminded them that the *BAJA 1000* blasted through that quiet desert outpost annually. Each photo or poster had a story to tell.

"Judging from this multitude of signed photos posted here, it looks like *Catavina* is a pivotal hub for the racing world, at least for a few days of the year." Reggie surmised. An International Off-road sporting event running through the *Baja California* peninsula, the event is one of the premiere races in the world, some even claimed *"the Mother of All Desert Races"*.

"Probably the biggest disruption of the year" Regina admonished obliquely. She shuddered to imagine the horror that such a spectacle would create for wildlife, as well as free-range cattle.

"The Missionaries could never have imagined an event like the *BAJA 1000* following in their footsteps?" Regina knew that the thought was preposterous, but comparing the tortuous path of the Sacred Expedition of 1769, on foot or donkey, with that of the road warriors of a contemporary contest like the *"1000",* was a paradox that couldn't be overlooked.

After ordering coffee and their favorite road-side meal, *Huevos Rancheros,* salsa over eggs, Regina wandered over to check the sparsely stocked souvenir counter. Jars of chili preserves led her to suppose that this was a local specialty. Other items constructed from the woven wooden core of cactus and a few decals didn't arouse much interest, but looking through a stack of postcards completely engaged her until the waiter returned with steaming mugs.

"There are some tasty treasures hidden in these mountains" she reported through the steamy cloud erupting from her mug, "and someone around here is sharing the treasure on hand crafted postcards."

The waiter hovered a bit, as he settled their plates on the table.

"Those are my postcards" he admitted to them in English.

Visitors forget that their conversations can often be understood by Mexicans. Spanish is the preferred language in BCS and it's always polite to begin conversations assuming that, but many Mexicans speak English or at least some Spanglish. Taken by surprise, Regina paused to re-evaluate the young man serving them.

He was handsome, yet unassuming, his gaze direct as he described the beauty of the landscapes hidden in the mountains around them. *Catvina* was his home, he explained but he had studied photography at University, returning with an expanded perspective and entrepreneurial skills. Empowered, he was channeling his creativity towards respect for the environment.

Standing in a shaft of light beaming through the ragged *palapa* roof, the seniors were mesmerized by the beauty that he described, realizing that they would have to be at least a decade younger to experience the remote scenery first hand. Altering their sense of wonder along that remote part of the *Camino Real,* it was an important reminder to not underestimate the power of youth and the creative spirit, wherever it comes to light.

Regina promised him that she would purchase each one of his beautiful postcards.

Back on the road, there was little traffic other than the occasional SUV loaded with kayaks and camping equipment. They did see riders on horseback though, weaving through the bizarre boulder-scape in a strangely parallel reality. A weird dichotomy of geology and illusion, it wasn't surprising that the area had evolved a mystique for travelers. One toke over the line, they could easily imagine space aliens waiting for them at the next scenic point.

A few kilometers north along the *camino,* an obscure turnout led to a shrine wedged between boulders as big as a house.

They had stopped at the small *mercado* in *Catavina* and purchased votive candles. It was for a ritual that they had maintained through the years; prayers to the Virgin de las Piedras - the Virgin of the Rocks. Painted on the wide rock face protected from the wind, the *Virgin de Guadalupe* sanctified the space, while a small inclosed alter below the image shielded offerings. *Yumano* and *Couchimi* petroglyphs in nearby caves had been radiocarbon dated to be 1000 to 6000 years old. Regina liked to fantasize that Serra himself had recognized the magical energy of the place. Many of her prayers there had been answered.

Surprising a large iguana, they continued to the shrine when it leaped back onto the desert.

"Hail Guadalupe, full of Grace... Blessed are thou among Sisters....Pray for us sinners..." she ritually recited, hoping for any random miracle.

"Especially forgiveness for the ones that leave behind their garbage" intoned Reggie, humoring his wife as he helped her light the candle, challenging with a sudden gust of wind.

Over the years they had grown accustomed to the litter and graffiti spread out along this stretch of the desert, but as they turned to round up the dogs, they suddenly realized that their prayer had already been answered.

"Es un milagro!"

Distracted by their conditioned reality, it took a miracle for the pilgrims to finally notice that the landscape had been changed. Litter was gone and the obnoxious graffiti had completely disappeared. Stunned, they turned to face the Virgin. With no explanation, she looked down on them blissfully from her stone portal.

"This is the miracle" Reggie tried to persuade Regina after he discovered a sign that they hadn't noticed on arrival.

"RESPECT THE NATURAL ENVIRONMENT!" Small print then explained that there would be a penalty of 60 hours of work removing graffiti from the rocks and picking up trash for any

violation. Whether anybody believed that the stones were sacred, or not, the environment was worthy of respect and the visitors were gratified to see the miraculous renewal of the natural landscape. The pilgrims couldn't help but wonder if the young waiter back in *Catavina* had anything to do with the miracle.

✦

The travelers were approaching the *Camino Real* settlement of *San Vincente* a hundred kilometers from *Ensenada* when Mr. Sniff and Ms. Chief signaled that it was time for a break. Travel advisors in tune with the real world, Reggie and Regina usually honored their instinctual advice. A small sign directed them to the turnoff for an historic mission. Scattered remnants of old olive orchards and vineyards suggested that the area had previously been a community with an extensive population.

"Looks like this site is under excavation" Reggie observed as he followed the dogs to the bushes.

Regina stretched into a few yoga postures as she studied a row of very gnarly cactus leading up a red earth hill. Two elderly crones were straightening up the plastic flowers, colorfully arranged around stacked stones in an ancient graveyard at the top of the hill. Waving as they greeted the arrival of visitors to the old mission site, their welcoming voices beckoned them like Angels, the daughters of the daughters calling them to witness.

"They seem to want to show us something, Reggie. *Vamos a ver*."

They entered the graveyard through a gate barely held together with an oblique collection of crooked sticks and pieces of barbed wire. In true *Baja* style, the rest of the fence defining the sacred space was a continuation of the same haphazard pattern.

"*Santa Maria...*" murmured Reggie as they approached the old *Señoras*. Beauty reflected from their smiling faces. Deep creases in their skin formed shiny kernels as firm as fresh husked corn. Little black eyes shone merrily from faces touched by time and the elements. They seemed to be in a state of joy in service to their dearly departed ancestors.

"...or maybe they are suspended in time?" Regina mused, trying to connect historical events to the present.

After the customary *"Como esta?"*, the visitors were beckoned to follow. Explaining enthusiastically with rapid gestures and pointing, the women led them down the other side of the hill to a vista point overlooking the jagged remains of an old Dominican mission. Emerging from the hillside, carefully excavated adobe walls, barely a meter high, outlined the extensive maze that had once been the center of an early *California* community. Behind them, the cheerful chatter of the angels faded into a meadow of wildflowers, leaving the pilgrims to explore on their own.

A valuable area of water and grazing at the important intersection of routes north to *Alta California* and east over the *Sierra Paso* leading to the *Colorado* river delta and mainland Mexico, *San Vincente* had been a strategic point on the *Camino Real*. Alongside the ruins of the mission were the ruins of an even larger military complex.

"....probably here to suppress resistance from local tribes and to control the converts held captive as labor for building the California Dream. Judging from the size of the jail, there must have been a lot of hostility" Reggie randomly speculated over the outline of the complex. "Water, grazing; there's bound to be confrontation over natural resources like these."

Beyond those crumbling walls of red adobe, the overgrown traces of the extensive irrigation system that had sustained the Dream was lightly etched into the terrain snaking through the valley below. The disciples of Jesus had come to save the innocent, then enslaved them to feed the chain of missions. Now the private farms of their descendants spread out like a vast mandala in all directions from the mission gardens.

Freshly painted plaques scattered among the ruins described *Dominican Padres* having founded Mission *San Vicente Ferrer* in 1780. It had soon developed into a vital link, becoming the administrative center for the Northern *Frontera*, headquarters for military troops guarding this strategic intersection through hostile *Pai-Pai t*ribal territory.

Curiously, they sifted through small piles of relics displayed along the walls. Old coins, buttons and hardwares were testimonials of the people that had been required to maintain this remote outpost.

"One person's garbage is another's treasure" Reggie surmised, holding up a shard of old pottery for closer scrutiny. "I wonder who is overseeing this excavation?"

"It's a miracle that The Conquest even made it this far." Years of exploring *Baja California* had sharpened Regina's respect for the strength of the elements. "Stick you, prick you, poke you! Then add thirst and hunger to that list of difficulties and it's no wonder that conquest was so brutal." It was strangely disorienting to be wandering among the ruins. This part of the Conquest had been reduced to a Scenic Point overgrown by the natural world.

"I wonder why this place fell into such disrepair after all the work of building it? Disease or disillusionment..." Regina mused, abstractedly tossing an ancient coin. "Heads or tails, Reggie?"

"Actually, the emergence of modern Mexico changed everything" Reggie explained, translating from the placard leaning against an old chunk of adobe at their feet. *"By freeing the native people who had worked and created the wealth for New Spain* and dividing the land among them, the missions lost their extensive holdings to privatization."

"Different times. Now *privatization* means corporate conquest." Straddling two worlds, Regina had to ponder on historical interpretation. "What a bizarre oxymoron."

Abandoning the ambiguity to resume their journey, they followed the path back through the ruins toward the cemetery. Insisting that they take a more direct route to the van and a bowl of water, Regina and Reggie allowed the dogs to lead them into an overgrown garden area, where it was easy for the four-legged travelers to slip under the barbed wire fencing, but not so easy for their two legged companions.

"Anyway, it was just too hot to climb back up the hill" Reggie reasoned agreeably. "So get on your knees Regina! If we have to go low, we may as well pray."

Humbled by the history surrounding them and the mistaken sound of dry grass beneath their knees, the supplicants were suddenly frozen by the appearance of a rattlesnake coiled to greet them on their path as it led under the rusty wire. "Don't move!" Reggie hissed. "Standing up right now might be misunderstood."

"Okay, I guess we'd better keep praying then" Regina continued as calmly as possible. She had facetiously been on her knees for Jesus, then faced with a messenger from the natural world, she really was praying for divine intervention.

Answered by ominous rattling, they spoke to the snake, explaining that they were not there in defiance. "We're just following the Path" they insisted, hoping that they weren't staring at immutable destiny.

"We're just a couple of old *gringos* heading home on the *Camino Real*... Oh Jesus!" Reggie pleaded convincingly.

Even as they spoke to it, they hoped that the snake had already figured out who they were. After all, there had been many other pilgrims before them. Without breaking eye contact, they continued to tell their story, any story, calmly and with intent. Blossoms wound through the barbed wire fence attracted unconcerned butterflies to flutter around them, while the sound of a raven's wing whispered its presence nearby, and the drone reached them from an airplane slowing in its approach to the airport in Tijuana.

The spell was broken by Ms.Chief, curiously returning to see what had happened to her posse. Nose to nose with the snake, the odds changed with her presence, but it still seemed like a miracle that the serpent quietly disappeared into the overgrown foliage of crimson *bougainvillea*.

"Better pray for another miracle..." Reggie grumbled, struggling to angle the van over the abrupt edge of the pavement with blind curves in both directions. "Visibility getting back on the *camino* could be a challenge."

"So, I'll look this way and you check that side" Regina suggested hopefully as Reggie revved up the engine. "Okay this direction" she reported.

It was probably only seconds until the van crept onto the pavement, but in those short seconds reality had totally changed. A gigantic fuel truck and trailer abruptly roared into view, ominously barreling towards them. Covered with dust and layers of dead bugs, its grillwork snarled at them with contempt. In that little space between breaths, Regina realized that Reggie was looking the other way.

"Stop!" she commanded urgently.

Time is so relative. The resonance from the giant truck penetrated their being at exactly the same moment that Reggie let up on the throttle, just enough for the rear wheel to slide back over the edge of the road and allow the phantom to pass in a ferocious blast of power.

Looking at each other in disbelief, they were speechless for a moment while the miracle of their quantum survival filtered into that special place of knowing.

"So now what should we do?" Taking a deep breath, Reggie was working up the courage for another attempt to reach the far side; just a few meters away, the illusive northbound lane seemed like a faraway mirage.

Remembering the historical challenge of travel along the *Camino Real*, Regina decided that Junipero Serra's personal motto might be appropriate for those following in his footsteps.

"Always forward, never back!" she quoted the old *Padre* who had forged a new path for *California*.

"Unless of course a hundred tons of diesel is heading straight at you" Reggie added with resilience.

After reaching the north bound lane of the highway, the resumption of their journey was uneventful until they rounded that first blind curve, and an iconic message materialized before them.

"CRISTO SALVA." Dust from the menacing Phantom was still settling over the *Camino,* as painted white rocks arranged across the hillside ahead of them eerily proclaimed Salvation.

The Conquest had moved on, leaving the spoils of victory to crumble. It had seemed like a testament to the futility of human endeavor, but now they weren't so sure.

The *Padres* had set high expectations for society during their reign, effecting the descendants of their converts in ways that reflected those standards. Following the path of the Sacred Expedition as it wove through the core of *California*, Reggie and Regina had witnessed enough miracles along the *Camino Real* that against all logic, they understood that the quantum mystery of faith lingered still through the spirit of the *Padres*

La Frontera

Wildflowers marched up the hilly slopes in wild procession of fragrance leading to *La Frontera:* Waves of orange poppies blended into purple lupines in spectacular vistas melting into fields of white, leaping to join the mounting cumulus billowing in from the Pacific. Mustard wound through the ravines like yellow rivers. Along the coast, St. Anne's Lace fringed the shoreline like breakers to the sand. The scent of *California* springtime in all its profusion was welcoming, as Reggie and Regina lingered along the path of their seasonal migration home.

"Are we ready?" The lingering look they exchanged said it all. The return to California USA was becoming more challenging every year.

After an almost thousand-mile drive with little traffic, it was getting congested as they neared the border separating old and new, *Alta y Baja California.* American foreign policy decisions made over recent decades have fueled massive displacement of Central Americans, many settling in the rich agricultural contours of the Baja Pacific coast, building communities and producing agricultural wealth for elites. Then after NAFTA agreements between Mexico and the U.S., *maquiladoras* - factories - erupted all along the border areas, attracting even more migration from all parts of Mexico and Central America to work making products for lucrative export. Spilling over onto the edges of the *Camino Real,* enterprising new entrepreneurs have created a melee of roadside distraction that has turned the border area into an obstacle course. Beginning at *San Quentin,* busses and farm equipment, pedestrians, stray dogs, potholes and the impact of mounting traffic, made for slow progress and there was good reason to be cautious. Not that travelers couldn't still find a few Scenic Points.

On a cultural level, Reggie and Regina always enjoyed the roadside vendors, the collective vignettes that make Mexico so unique. Rustic structural configurations virtually made them feel like they were visiting booths at the Renaissance Faire. Welcoming shoppers with a wide variety of specialty products *Made in Mexico,* local farm produce, pottery, wood, copper and fiber products added to the similarities. They had deliberately packed light for the trip back to the States, leaving plenty of space for camping gear and the dogs, but now they were ready to load up. Dodging busses pulling on and off the *Camino Real* haphazardly, the Dodge Ram meandered along slowly in a parade of muddy vehicles, making them vulnerable to impulse shopping.

An intricately woven cradle basket for a soon to arrive grandchild was Regina's first purchase and she was able to tuck smaller baskets inside of that. Colorful Mexican blankets always made iconic gifts, plus made good packing for unique ceramic totems and a huge ceramic bowl. Regina insisted that Reggie wedge a couple of crooked chairs between the kayaks tied to the roof of the van. Of course they always brought jars of honey and vanilla back for friends and family. And Reggie was always ready to feast on fresh oysters.

Drifting over to a friendly vendor with tables in front of a counter heaped with oysters on ice, he and Regina were preparing to get intimate with a plate of mollusks when, they were interrupted by a chorus of greeting.

"Noooort! Noooort!" It was C.Nick Point with his cousin Vista. He loved oysters as much as Reggie did, so it was no mystery.

"Thought you would still be recovering from your surgeries" Regina exclaimed in amazement. They knew that Vista was donating one of her kidneys to her cousin.

"Not yet. We want to finish one quest before beginning another...." Vista Point explained tentatively, raising questions that needed to be asked.

"Are you afraid you won't be back after the transplant?" Regina was concerned about their friends. Everywhere they went, they would always find C.Nic Point and she couldn't imagine travels along the *Camino Real* without the expectation of those happy connections.

"No way! I plan on spending more time here in the future, not less. There's still so much more that I want to explore." Nic's response was reassuring. "We're on a quest." Pausing to squeeze lime on another oyster, Nic carefully dripped Tabasco before explaining.

"Before we go under the knife, I want to share a *Baja* adventure with Vista." Offering the prepared delicacy to his cousin, she opened her mouth wide while Nic delicately tipped the slippery mollusk over the edge. "I want to bring Vista to the Tropic of Cancer while there are still wonders to behold. I think we can get to the dunes in San Quentin by sunset."

"But hey, a quest is sometimes like stepping into an abyss..." Reggie obliquely reminded his *amigo*.

"We've traveled to many countries around the world together, but I've never explored *Baja California* with Nic. I've heard so many stories, and now I want to understand his fascination." Vista was describing a common compulsion. From the Friars to the Snowbirds, visionaries had been dreaming *California* for centuries.

"The *Camino Real* is the highway to adventure and even more; a journey through living history, yet at the same time a place of ultra-real time" Reggie explained sliding another slimy morsel onto his tongue. His chin was dripping with lime and *tabasco* as he finished his thought with a parable. "Baja is becoming one big burrito wrapped in a golden metaphor, gushing with *Salsa Picante!*"

At that point Reggie and Nic went into an orgy of consumption, quickly devouring the rest of the oysters on the plate while signaling for more. Saltine cracker crumbs were flying from their mouths like confetti as they shared information about road conditions and military check points, leaving Vista and Regina to share other concerns.

"I want to swim with the whales if they're still around, and turtles are totem beings for me." Vista started reciting her list of expectations, while Regina meticulously prepared another shellfish. thinking "she's talking like this is a trip to Disneyland", contemplating whether or not she should clarify current circumstances.

"Things are happening in *Baja* that are difficult to explain..." she trailed off. Regina was struggling to define her own growing disillusionment without deflating Vista's enthusiasm.

"I recently counted 88 dead turtles along the East Cape. PROFEPA reported that it was a red tide, but it could also have been something illegal, like net fishing. The Sea is being over fished. The locals don't want to admit it, but environmental rules and quotas are being ignored for the sake of tourism. *Baja Cali-*

fornia is materializing the tension between dreams and unwelcome new realities...." Regina slumped uncomfortably as she told the story.

Luckily a pair of fucking dogs became a timely distraction. Copulating on the muddy shoulder of the nearby *camino*, it was hilarious to see them creating the kind of ribald entertainment that the moment required.

Vista sputtered, raising her bottle of *cerveza* in a provocative gesture.

"Here's to serendipity then! That will be good enough."

Met by a chorus of "Norts!" they all joined her in a toast to the unexpected as the fucking dogs proceeded to roll toward their table of oysters and a continuing concert of laughter. Only Regina knew that she was also laughing at herself for underestimating Vista Point.

Taking into consideration C.Nic Point's information that the road to the border crossing at *Tecate* was a muddy mess of construction projects, Reggie had decided to make the crossing at *Tijuana's San Ysidro* Port of Entry instead.

Cruising along the scenic toll road toward *Tijuana*, far above the wide panorama of the glimmering Pacific horizon, it was impossible to speculate where Mexico ended and the United States began. First explored by Cabrillo in 1542, rampant Real Estate development along the expanding coastal communities was a growing sign of foreign occupation. An invasion of newcomers was building an impressive diversity of architectural achievements adapted to coastal living around yacht harbors and managed estates. *Rosarita* Beach had become well known as a wedding destination. The lagoons of *La Mision* were crowded with kayaks. Reggie and Regina wondered which ones were homes for the notorious Tijuana Cartel?

Hints of a kaleidoscope sunset were gathering over the rolling breakers along the *Playas de Tijuana,* when the Ram abruptly collided with the ragged edge of an emerging reality. Traffic! Backed up along the battered border fencing, dented and heavily plastered with graffiti describing human desperation, they had to look away from the slumped figure of a man shooting up right there on the sacred edge of the world.

"*Pinche* welcome to the Land of *Opportunidad*" Reggie cringed, merging into the sluggish line-up crawling to the Port of Entry. A path of red taillights followed the wall while *Tijuana* unfolded below them in a phantasmagorical heap of chunky hot sauce.

Originally dreamed of as a commercial gateway into Mexico, *Tijuana* has earned a reputation as a hub of colorful shopping experiences, entertainment and classical cultural perversion. A Border Industrialization Program later intensified the explosion of growth associated with manufacturing, creating a hub for migration. Erupting from the center of the city, *Tijuana* had consumed the surrounding hills and canyons with *maquiladoras,* shopping malls, supermarkets, bars, schools, museums and growing neighborhoods of cardboard and corrugated metal squatter shacks climbing uphill to the cell towers dominating the skyline. Coming to life in the growing dusk, the city sparkled like a Christmas tree.

Hypnotized by the glitter, Reggie's sudden swerve to avoid hitting a desperate family of pedestrians, jolted them back to consciousness. Dodging erratically between traffic, a man dragging two young children, followed by a very pregnant woman loaded with bundles, reached the ragged edge of the border and dissolved through a purple slit hidden under a sign advertising travel insurance. The abrupt detour accidentally led the Ram into a confusing vortex.

"That sign says we are on our way to San Felipe and that one pointing the same way says *Zona Centro*..... Reggie!" Regina was perplexed as her partner recklessly steered towards the center of a giant meltdown.

"Just following the path with heart" he replied apologetically, pointing to a red neon Valentine flashing like a beacon from the window of an otherwise shabby edifice.

"Hearts?" Regina had to wonder if they were in the red-light district.

By the next block, *catinas* throbbing with *mariachi* music spilled out onto sidewalks crowded with taco stands and vendors carrying stacks of merchandise, all competing for attention along with street entertainers and a spray painted 'zonkey' on every corner. That was when surrender began.

"So, what's Sponge Bob telling us?" Floating like a superhero emerging from the throbbing sunset, a big inflated *Bob Esponja* seemed to be inviting them to join the fun of a cultural megalopolis; rich and poor, old and young, a cosmopolitan dichotomy dripping with the chaos of reckless capitalism. *Tijuana*. Eventually finding themselves under the tall Millennial Arch on *Avenida Revolution,* it became full emersion in a city of metaphor: California Dreaming, resistance had become futile.

When the *gringos* from the East Cape finally surfaced for a reality check, they were hoping that the line-up for border crossing might be less chaotic.

Signed on February 2, 1848, the *Treaty of Guadalupe Hidalgo* had ceded 55% of its territory to the United States, including all or parts of Arizona, California, New Mexico, Texas, Wyoming, Colorado, Nevada and Utah, promising freedom of access after the Mexican/American War. Article one had described a "*Treaty of Peace and Friendship"*, but the early twentieth-first century crawl to customs at the border had instead become intimidating.

"... *in general, all persons whose occupations are for the common subsistence and benefit (of the people), shall be allowed to continue their respective employments unmolested in their persons"* further reads the treaty, but the politically divided United States had tightened its borders after 9-11, creating long waits when crossing, especially at *Tijuana*.

Trying to squeeze into the column of traffic leading up to the Port of Entry, they were immediately approached by a uniformed officer demanding a fine for cutting in. After that was settled, he directed the *gringos* to the end of the line-up, which became a confusing route of one-way streets teeming with more shopping opportunities. Still slightly under the influence of *Margarita*, at one point they were almost convinced by a fast-talking *Tijuanero*, that they could get their van painted for just $300!

As the hours passed, the crawl to the border became excruciating.

"This is hypnotic," Reggie admitted, "and tell me why I thought this would be an easier crossing?" They loved the scenic routes, but shopping had lost its entertainment value. "Maybe it's not even about Scenic Points after all.....?"

"How about another Hot Dog?" Regina suggested, signaling a young vender with a baby bundled on her back.

"So sad to see a baby on the night shift..." she uttered sadly to her partner. Handing over a big tip - which was probably the reason why the baby was brought along anyway - a young child then came up to her window asking if she needed to use his family's toilet, for a dollar.

"Who is more pitiful?" she had to ask herself. History had written that Padre Junipero Serra, the Franciscan Father of California had hoped to help the 'pitiful people', and now she found herself also hoping to help them, even as she was feeling pity for herself. With the fluid character of music drifting from the audios surrounding them, it should have been a party, but stuck for hours in a vehicle breathing air thick with exhaust from idling traffic, she wasn't feeling very festive about their return.

When the migrating Snowbirds finally joined one of the eighteen lanes spread out in front of the gateway to freedom, Regina was ready to light up an oily little roach that she had discovered while searching through her backpack for her passport.

"Are you crazy" Reggie exploded, "there are surveillance cameras everywhere!"
Just then an officer leading a sniffing dog appeared a couple of lanes over, so Regina quickly ate it.

Entering the zone of surveillance, Reggie also noticed something else.

"Looks like we've reached the beggar zone" he commented sadly.

Just a dozen vehicles from the gate, a one legged elder on crutches held out her gnarly hands, pleading for something to eat. Kissing her rosary, she was grateful for the hot dog that Reggie handed over. Behind her, a man in a wheelchair with no legs straddled the divide between cars, hoping for a miracle. Barely reacting to the *pesos* that Reggie tossed into his *sombrero,* they each knew that it would never be enough. The poverty existing in the midst of prosperity brought them painful clarity as the Dodge Ram received the green light to pull into the kiosk at customs.

"Do you have anything to declare? Are you transporting any fresh agricultural products?" The Customs Official seemed distracted as he looked over their passports, but when Reggie automatically answered "No", Regina cringed.

"Do you mind if I inspect your cooler?" the officer inquired, pointing through the window into an interior packed with new merchandise and camping gear.

Finding a lemon floating around in the cooler of *Topo Chico* mineral water and melted ice, they were directed to Lane "W" for further scrutiny. Following instructions, they got out of the van with the dogs to wait on a bench with a view of the action.

"Not exactly scenic, but at least we've made it as far as the Group "W" bench" Reggie spoofed satirically. It was a *Baby Boomer* generational reference that Regina didn't think was so funny at the time.

The scene became increasingly surreal. Starting to feel the influence of the oily little roach that she had swallowed twenty minutes before, Regina couldn't get comfortable: She was thirsty; the lights were too bright; the air was heavy with fumes; it was noisy from the squeal of spinning tires making their rapid escapes.

As the senior suspects tried to make themselves invisible on the hard metal bench, a shiny new LEXUS was parking nearby. An inspection officer opening the trunk shouted for assistance as three fugitives bolted into view, each scattering in a different direction. One of the *desperados* making a frantic dash for freedom ran straight down the "W" lane towards them. Igniting a wild chorus of barking from Mr. Sniff and Ms. Chief, they were freaked to watch a giant Shephard dog jump on his back, knocking him to the ground. Landing right in front of them, a frightened youth looked up with a nosebleed dripping onto the pavement. Pleading for help with eyes brimming with tears, they suddenly realized that the fugitive was a young woman and it seemed shameful to watch her being roughly restrained with one officer holding her to the ground with his boot while they shackled her wrists. Shutting down the border while she was being apprehended, the other two fugitives had somehow disappeared back through the border into Mexico.

"Welcome to the California Dream...." Reggie mumbled as she was being led away. "Only sometimes it can be a nightmare" he had to solemnly conclude.

"Wow!" What ever happened to the *Treaty of Peace and Friendship?*" Regina was struck dumb with compassion, staring at the smeared blood on the grimy pavement below them. The incident had altered her consciousness. This wasn't part of her California dream.

As a Surf Safari van of young people of all colors and all with gnarly dreads parked down the line, they couldn't help but gape while they unloaded their entire van of sandy surf gear, spreading even their soiled underwear on the pavement for inspection.

"*Santa Maria,* aren't you glad we don't fit that profile?"

But Regina wasn't feeling as confident. "What are the chances, but there's still a chance?" she had to remind him. "It's almost midnight, we're not through this yet and I'm not exactly feeling exceptional."

Then some kind of altercation erupting on the Tijuana side closed the border for another twenty minutes. Still feeling invisible as Federal Officers reacted to each episode, the Snowbirds had been perched for an hour waiting for their inspection, hesitant to tempt serendipity with complaint.

It was then that they abruptly understood that it wasn't simply serendipity: Misplaced nationalism was threatening a mutually beneficial, historic relationship, dimming the California Dream on both sides of the border with fear and uncertainty.

When Reggie and Regina finally left their confiscated lemon behind to join traffic speeding up the *Camino Real* into San Diego, they were still pondering their own translation of the California Dream.

Padre California

Regina arrived early to discover that the parking lot at *San Carlos de Borromeo de Carmelo* was already full. The fog was lifting as she pulled into a space down the hill from the old mission, close to a public path alongside a small stream.

"Probably the source of irrigation for the Mission gardens" she supposed, inspecting the slope up to the old edifice. A lineup of day-glow cones dividing the highway was seemingly the only evidence that history and destiny would soon be crossing.

That afternoon's Canonization of Franciscan Friar Junipero Serra, would be making Carmel the ecclesiastic capitol of California. Regina was impelled to be there, not only because of her own interest in California history, but also in memory of a favorite Aunt who had grown up in the historic Monterey community.

The fog had been thick earlier that morning along coastal Highway 1 to Monterey, bestowing a mystical quality to hazy memories from Regina's youth, stories of old Mission days from Aunt Josephine de Carli. Not really a blood relative, rather a lifetime neighbor and close family friend, out of respect for the kindred spirit that they shared, they always called her Auntie Carli. She had been a lifelong educator, slender and stooped with thick lens glasses and she had always announced herself with a high decibel greeting.

"Yoooo hoooo!" And she was a storyteller.

"After school we would mount the horse, a massive gray workhorse, too old to work the fields anymore, and my two sisters and I would ride down the beach to be with Grandfather while he did chores around the Mission."

"Grandfather's farm adjoined the Mission." Auntie Carli would always repeat her story in the same way, so that it would be remembered, Regina supposed.

"A very old Native woman who had grown up at the Mission, kept history alive with stories of the beloved Friar of her youth." Said to be congenial, zealous and sincere, "Junipero Serra had used song and ritual to evangelize. "Oh..." Auntie would reminisce, "she told my young Grandfather how people flocked to hear the Friar sing Mass."

Regina had heard the story many times. She liked to imagine a young Josephine whenever she passed that red schoolhouse, still stubbornly anchored on Monastery Beach along Highway 1, close to the Mission. In sight of Point Lobos, that beach was also where Auntie's great-grandfather, a Portuguese whaler, had kept his launch. Because of those stories, the place had become a magical landmark for Regina, a place of spirits scattered among crumbling whale skeletons: Old Gray with the three sisters plodding down the foggy shoreline to the mission, forever....

"The old woman had also told my Grandfather where the Friar was buried" Auntie would go on to clarify.

So it was Josephine de Carli's grandfather, Cristiano Machado, who finally had led the papal authorities to Junipero Serra's grave. Buried in rubble beneath the mission edifice, the Mission had been abandoned since Secularization had redistributed mission lands in 1834. After the historic discovery, it became Cristiano's passion to work on restoration projects around the Mission.

It was usually about then in the storytelling that Auntie Carli would bring out 'The Relic'. During the process of exhumation, her grandfather had pocketed a chunk from Serra's coffin, and it had later become a holy relic for his grand-daughter. Regina remembered how Auntie would un-wrap it carefully and gently place the magical piece of wood in her hands and insist that she hold it for a while.

"Maybe, she thought it would cure my psoriasis..." Regina contemplated, "and maybe I should have been a better believer. Now that the Friar is being declared a Saint, that crusty chunk of coffin might actually have had miraculous power! If only Auntie could have been here today..."

On a spiritual level, maybe she was.

Shifting her attention back up the hillside to the Mission, Regina imagined the gardens that must have flowered there during Franciscan times. Like their Patron Saint, Francis of Assisi, the Franciscan friars had worked the fields alongside the mission converts. Stories and historical ledgers chronicled a thriving Christian community of hundreds around Carmel. She relished that sense of historical presence, even though the gardens had long been covered by houses and asphalt, realizing at the same time that the garden had been the beginning of the agricultural phenomena that had eventually expanded to feed a nation.

Winding her way up the hill through a maze of early 21st century vehicles, Regina wasn't surprised to discover a press conference taking place at the front gate, only she hadn't expected it to be a gathering of Native Americans being interviewed.

The descendants of the indigenous native ancestors were all dressed in black. Additional fashion statements of silver, turquoise and stone jewelry, fur and leather, beaded vests, frilled jackets and feathered adornments with iconic patterning, further defined tribal affiliation and status. Some were wearing moccasins, although most footwear ironically tended to be contemporary, athletic name brands. Many had been walking for days and even weeks, traveling from all around America on a sacred quest of their own. An officious looking elder wearing a full feather headdress posed proudly with an ornately carved wooden staff was describing his journey from Arizona. Now gathering in tribal support at the Canonization, they weren't there in celebration, but in protest.

"I have come here to honor my People" he declared solemnly. Listening to grievances from the protesters, Regina was saddened by allegations of slavery, brutal punishments such as whipping, involuntary segregation and harsh suppression of native languages and customs endured by their ancestors. Their shields that day were hand printed signs of disapproval.

"Junipero Serra was not a Saint, he was a monster!"

Giggling Coyote was shifting sorely from foot to foot, describing her exhausting pilgrimage with friends, walking on foot all the way from Mission Sonoma, the most northern of the Mission chain.

"I walked here so that the truth can be told." She and her companions referenced the truth as coming from a book called 'Crown of Thorns'.

A heavily beaded man wearing a faded black cap had come from the Santa Clarita Valley in Southern California. Describing himself as a *Tataviam*, he showed no mercy while relating the sad history of his tribe.

"My people lived on slopes facing the sun, existing harmoniously with nature along the Pacific Coast until our land and our toil were forcibly conscripted to build the Mission Empire." His long braids shook wildly with the passion of his story.

"The Sacred Expedition had tragically included many unrealistic expectations" Regina was reminded. "Cruel irony, the Friars claimed they had come to save...." Watching the press conference while most visitors filtered through the Holy gates to await the Canonization, protest wasn't something that she'd been expecting.

The Canonization would be telecast live at noon from the Basilica of the Immaculate Conception in Washington D.C., where Pope Francis would officially confirm Friar Junipero Serra as the first American Saint. A Costanoan tribal elder from the Esselen Nation announced that a ceremony honoring their Indigenous ancestors was planned to coincide.

Passing through the thick wooden gates of the sanctuary, Regina could see that the grounds had been immaculately groomed for the occasion, with an abundance of colorful flowers flooding around what she recognized as native varieties of cacti from Baja California. Wandering into the courtyard, a life-sized bronze of the Friar who had brought Christianity to California, reached for more souls from beneath a gnarly old pepper tree. Behind him, a small adobe building beckoned.

After the brightness of the courtyard, dim museum lighting reinforced the effect of stepping back a couple of centuries, as she was drawn into the cool adobe structure. Met by a display of native baskets and bead and shell necklaces, the simplicity of native arts and customs was a timely beginning to the chronicle. Then she recognized a photo of Auntie Carli's grandfather, Christiano Machado, leaning back against the centuries. Although the official story credited Sir Harry Downie for the restoration, Auntie had told of how her grandfather's labor had helped with restoration after President Abraham Lincoln returned the missions to the Franciscans in 1865. For Regina, the relics told a familiar story.

Requisitioned objects brought from the Baja missions were displayed, along with a running historical commentary. Finding herself alone with these relics of California history, Regina experienced a sense of time travel as she recalled her own adventures along the King's Highway.

After establishing the first missions in *San Fernando de Velicata* and *San Diego* while enduring many delays, hardships and desertions, the various arms of the Sacred Expedition had converged at the Bay of *Monte Rey* on 1 June 1770. Fifty-four years old when he joined the expedition, *Padre Presidente* Junipero Serra had arrived aboard the supply ship San Antonio to rendezvous with the overland contingent led by California Governor Don Gaspar de Portola. Together they founded the Presidio/Mission *San Carlos Borromeo,* raising the Spanish flag and erecting a Cross under the same tree at the harbor of Monterey where Sebastian Vizcaino had claimed California for Spain fifteen decades earlier.

Amazing the indigenous peoples with the pompous ceremony of their arrival, the flaunting of Christian images and artifacts, all requisitioned from the *Baja* missions, singing of Mass and ringing of bells, along with enough cannon and rifle fire to make a strong impression, it had been a hopeful beginning for the Spanish occupation. Then it had been up to the Franciscans to prepare the gentiles for a new way of life as citizens of Spain and the military made it clear that there would be no other options.

But by August of 1771, bad relations between the Native converts and the military, including rape, brutality and murder, forced *Padre Presidente* Serra to relocate the Mission.

He chose a new location with fertile land that was five miles south, along the banks of the Carmel River. Inspired by the example of Saint Francis of Assisi, founder of the Franciscan Order, the hopeful Friar took up the task of creating a self-sustaining, Christian community. Setting up gardens and planting the seeds brought from *Baja California,* Serra was determined to foster a *Nuevo California* with the help of the friendly natives that he'd enticed to the Mission.

Along with Carmel, three more missions were founded nearby in that same year, but mistreatment of the natives by soldiers continued to be a problem and relations with the *Presidio Commandante* became strained. By the next year, Padre Serra was forced to make a strenuous trip to Mexico City to petition the Viceroy of New Spain to support human rights for the Indigenous People of California. Importantly at that time, Serra submitted a thirty-two-point ***Representacion,*** a Bill of Rights for Californians. Adopted on the first of January 1774, the document redefined Military/Mission relations, placing civilian welfare exclusively under Franciscan control. Further, the petition increased the supplies of food, animals and emigrants to the California missions. Serra then returned to *Nueva California* to continue the expansion of the mission chain, in all founding nine missions and baptizing over 6000 new converts before his death in 1784

Wandering back into the 21st Century, Regina was still thinking about Christian expansion when she literally bumped into Giggling Coyote. Distracted as their paths crossed, they were both examining gravestones along the side of the chapel that had been repaired and propped up in remembrance of the faithful. Leaning at an angle before them, "Old Gabriel" must have been one of those.

"Those are my people over there" Coyote volunteered, pointing to a dusty graveyard in the shadows alongside the Basilica. "Once they were baptized, they were not allowed to leave the Mission Community."

"Maybe they wanted to be here," Regina responded impulsively. "My family stories say that Friar Serra was beloved by the converts. He protected them like a father. Before Serra's Bill of Rights, the military was out of control abusing the natives"

"Who is your family?" Caught off guard, Coyote responded curiously.

Regina was friendly as she explained her ancestral connections, while Coyote compared her own. Saints or monsters, gazing through the eyes of their ancestors, it was soon obvious that they were at an impasse when they were saved by a summons. Requisitioned for the Sacred Expedition from the mission in *Loreto,* and brought to Monterey, the chapel bell was calling the faithful to Mass.

The bell also tolled for the Indigenous, signaling the beginning of the Native Tribute. The people in black were gathering quietly in preparation, sweeping the naked earth of their tribal forebears and rearranging the abalone shells hanging from rough wooden crosses. Coyote's companions were tugging on her sleeve as they called her for their ritual.

Departing with a note of sadness, "Never named.... our graves are marked only by shells," Coyote returned to her people.

Along with the faithful and the curious, Regina lingered in the spiritual after-Mass, magnetically drawn to the historical moment and the presence of so many antiquities. Studying Saint

Joseph, the three-foot tall, titular Patron of the Expedition, she couldn't help wondering if his downcast eyes weren't a subtle call for submission? Mesmerized by the Cloth of Gold worn by the notoriously pious Padre Serra, she finally decided that the glittering vestment had probably been incorporated for spectacle. Hanging behind glass, it was made from Chinese silk.

"*....I soon had the opportunity of showing it to advantage on the Solemnity of Corpus Christi.*" Serra had written in thanks to the Viceroy for the gift. "*We made a great event of it this year.*"

"Oh, right! Saint Junipero was an eighteenth century rock star...?" In hindsight, Regina couldn't help making the comparison. She had known that Serra loved music, but she was amused to also think of him as a choreographer, blending music and flash to produce events that would attract new converts to Christianity.

Inspecting the remaining fragments of the Saint's coffin, also protected under glass, Regina wondered if the small chunk of wood bundled on top was Auntie Carli's holy relic? It was possible, since her Aunt's Catholic relatives had demanded the relic after her death.

Then following the altar rail from the coffin of the Saint, she encountered the sweet face of Our Lady of Bethlehem, gazing down from the altar. Framed by pillars of gold, she had been donated by the Archbishop of Mexico City as "Conquistadora", Conquerer of Souls. Struck by the irony that Mary and her Baby Jesus had led the Conquest of California, Regina pondered the paradox of her sweet masque. Intuitively sensing from the look of pity raining down on humanity from the Lady's downcast eyes, she might have known the outcome of glorified promise would be predictable disappointment.

Emerging from the mystical, Regina came to the grave of the soon-to-be Saint, flanked by the remains of fellow missionaries, Juan Crespi and Fermin de Lausen, laying side-by-side beneath the floor of stone. It was this trio of Franciscan Brothers from Spain who had established Christianity in *Nueva California*. Along with a host of other ecclesiastic and historical considerations, their dreams and tenacity had changed the destiny of California.

"Always go forward..." had been Junipero Serra's motto and Regina felt the power of his determination as she considered the wealth that had spread out over the Golden State. Called the Father of California, the farm animals and seeds that he'd brought with the Sacred Expedition had implicitly changed California from a hunter-gatherer culture into an agrarian society. The abundance sparked by the missions, now feeding a nation, was a profound legacy.

"... and never go back" Serra's motto had concluded.

Completion of construction projects along *El Camino Real* in the late 20th century had finally connected California and new patterns of trade and migration were creating adventure and opportunities for new generations following the Kings Highway, with historic implications. Attracted by golden promises, new waves of colonization had brought ex-pats, snowbirds and investors from all over the world, again competing for sparse desert resources. Big money, luxury hotels and condominium developments were surrounding the mission towns and gobbling up pristine beach-front property. Just as they had displaced the indigenous communities before them, the new colonialists were globalizing the Mexican culture with new food choices, pharmaceuticals, corporate imports and expanded travel options for tourists and elites, still dreaming California.

The giant Jumbotron screen, set up in the courtyard, left no doubt that Junipero Serra would now be taking his message into a whole new dimension, through an intimidating web of heavy electrical cords generating a leap into Sainthood. Several hundred chairs were set up in front of the screen, but most people were milling around the sacred grounds, waiting for the Pope to begin the ceremony. Regina was sitting on the side lines watching AL JAZEER Television interview a talking head, when a woman joined her on the wide rock wall.

"Welcome!" It was the President of the Docent Association. Festively dressed in floral print, she was exuberant.

"Thank you. Glad we're connecting for such an historic occasion." Regina went on to briefly explain her reasons for coming. Going on to mention that she had not seen a caption with the photo of Christiano Machado in the little adobe museum, her new acquaintance became curious.

"I guess you know then, that Christiano was the caretaker of the mission when Serra was first exhumed?"

Admitting that it was family history, Regina reminded her that it was he that had known the location of Serra's grave.

"Then you'll probably be interested to know we've just completed a six million dollar earthquake retro-fit. Why don't you come to one of our meetings to share your story…"

Regina didn't get a chance to respond. Jewel Gentry, the California missions Coordinator rushed up just then to introduce some visitors from Europe. Looking very royal in purple, the docent led them off for a quick tour, while Jewel went to check on the simulcast, which was starting to flicker.

Taking a seat in the sun facing the giant screen, Regina surrendered to the spectacle and pageantry of the event, thinking how the Saint might have been impressed by the production. Broadcasting real time from across the continent, Pope Francis called on all the Saints for their blessing on the Canonization as he addressed the cyber world.

"We all know the struggle of glum apathy. How do we create the joy? Tread the dusty roads of history" the Pope preached. *"Go out to people of all nations to proclaim the joy of the gospel!"* Speaking in Spanish, the Pope was honoring Latino Catholics in all the Americas, while he characterized Junipero Serra as an openhearted man who had sought to protect Native Americans from colonial abuse.

The Plaza broke into applause as the Pope said the words of Confirmation and the bells of *San Carlos de Borromeo del Rio Carmelo* rang out with the news. Cameras scanned the angelic faces of the choir while the orchestra played music picked from the times that would have been familiar to the Saint. Feeling the spirit, Regina imagined what this ceremony would have meant to her very Catholic Aunt, who had testified years earlier during the process of Beatification.

"Go to those who have lost the joy and heal the wounds" the Pope commanded, raising his arms in the name of the Holy Spirit.

The homily of Pope Francis moved Regina's heart with compassion to contemplate the Tribes gathered on the far side of the Basilica, mourning the legacy of Conquest. They were so close, but healing seemed so far away.

Still Dreaming California

Appendix

A plaque was tacked to an old Pepper tree in the Indian Cemetery at *San Carlos de Borromeo del Rio Carmelo* sometime after the Canonization of St. Junipero Serra:

In memory of the Christian Indians interned in this cemetery of unmarked graves at the Mission San Carlos Borromeo in Carmel, California.
These symbolic grave sites adorned with abalone shells, represent the many hundreds of indigenous people buried in this graveyard and beyond. May they be honored, and may we be reminded of their long term presence, their rich culture and humanity and the importance that they still hold for their descendants today.

Still Dreaming California is an original work by Laurie Anderson Hennig. It does include references to information commonly known, but any resemblance to other published information is coincidental. The books listed here are recommended reading for anyone interested in the profound history and experience of California.

1. Barbara, Jack, and Patty Williams, "The Magnificent Peninsula, The Comprehensive Guidebook to Mexico's Baja California", 1998
2. Harry W. Crosby, "Antigua California Missions and Colony on the Peninsular Frontier", University of New Mexico Press, Albuquerque, 1697 -1768, published in 1994
3. Henry D Barrows, and, Luther A. Ingersoll, "Memorial and Biographical History of The Coast Counties of Central California", The Lewis Publishing Co., Chicago,1893
4. Rose Marie Beebe and Robert M. Senkewicz, Editors, "Lands of Promise and Despair, Chronicles of Early California", 1535-1846, edited in 2001
5. Fray Francisco Palou, O.F.M., "Historical Memoirs of New California, V1", Edited by Herbert Eugene Bolton, University of California Press, 1926
6. Fermin Francisco de Lasuen, "Writings of Fermin Francisco de Lasuen", Translated and edited by Finbar Kenneally, O.F.M., William Byrd Press, 1965
7. Martin J. Morgado, "A Pictorial Biography", Siempre Adelante Publishing, 1991
8. Padre James Donald Francez, "The Lost Treasures of Baja California", Black Forrest Press, 1996

Still Dreaming California

Laurie Anderson Hennig is an artist living with her artist husband in the mountains above the Monterey Bay of California. Both raised in Salinas California, with family connections to stories of early California history, curiosity led them to explore legends down *El Camino Real*, The Royal Highway, the heart of California, annually since their first visit there in 1980. As 'Snowbirds' drawn to mild winters as well as historical mystique, they have become a part of the cultural metamorphosis challenging the modern political divide of the California Republic.

Made in the USA
Columbia, SC
02 December 2022